SEALing the DEAL

Episode #2 of The Kapahu Series

By

L. D. K. Johnson

Sale of this book without a front cover may be unauthorized. If this book is coverless, it may have been reported to the publisher as "**unsold** or **destroyed**" and neither the author nor the publisher may have received payment for it.

Copyright © 2013 by L. D. K. Johnson

All rights reserved. No portion of this book may be reproduced in any form without permission from the publisher Belen Books, LLC., except as permitted by U.S. copyright law.

For permission, contact **Belen Books, LLC**.

This is a work of fiction. Names, characters, businesses, places, events, locales, and incidents are either the products of the author's imagination or used in a fictitious manner. Any resemblance to actual people, living or dead, sexy SEALS in uniform (or out of them), and or actual events or places is purely coincidental.

ISBN: 978-1-959715-27-6

Library of Congress Control Number: **2023948343**
Published by **Belen Books, LLC**
St. Petersburg, FL | Winter Park, FL | Chicago, IL USA
Belenbookspublishing.com

Edited by Beverly R. Waalewyn & Paul Hight
Cover by Belen Media Group

10 9 8 7 6 5 4 3 2

 Printed in the United States of America

For All the

Men and Women

in uniform.

SEALing THE DEAL

THE KAPAHU SERIES

CHAPTER ONE

Lieutenant Commander Koa Kapahu laughed unmercifully at the other officer walking sullenly beside him. The other man's usually bright gray-blue eyes were tinged red like he'd been out drinking all night, but Koa knew it was Aiden's eight-week-old daughter, Aria, keeping him up at night.

"Nah, brah." The 6'7", dark-haired, *WWE* wrestler-sized, Dwayne *'The Rock'* Johnson look-alike smiled at his brother-in-law, Lieutenant Aiden Kaplan, his hazel eyes sparkling mischievously. "My sister is never gonna go for that idea."

"I need the rest, man," Aiden stated matter-of-factly, looking around before speaking again. "And I need some… *you know*… alone time with your sister."

Koa grimaced, and the lunch he had eaten several hours previously threatened to evacuate his churning stomach.

"Dude," he stated in a hushed tone. "Don't talk about Kai and sex in the same sentence. It makes me itchy to think of you and my little sister having—"

"Sex," Aiden whispered back.

"Ugh, don't say it." Koa felt his skin actually starting to itch. "Don't even think about it if you can."

"Hey!" Aiden challenged the obviously grossed-out Navy SEAL. "Can I help it if I married the sexiest woman on the face of the planet and wanna *'bow-chicka-bow-wow'* with her—"

"Oh, God! Oh, God!" Koa screeched like a horned owl. "You're going to melt my ears off my head."

"Sorry," Aiden chuckled at the other man's discomfort. "I'll try not to mention Kai or sex in the same sentence anymore. Okay? You big baby. Who knew such a large man could be such a big pussy."

Koa's brows rose.

"Since you're not getting any pussy then you can't call me that," Koa grinned impishly.

Aiden shook his head in frustration.

"C'mon Koa, watch the kids for us this weekend," he pleaded. "I just want some alone-time with my wife without interruptions. A.J. would love spending time with his uncle, and Aria, well Aria just eats, sleeps, and poops right now, but she's so cute and cuddly and—"

"Stop! Just stop! If Kai agrees to it, I'll do it." Koa shook his head. "I'll watch my niece and nephew so you can get your balls back. Being a husband and father is really turning you into a wimp."

Truth was, his younger sister, Kai, and Aiden were basically newlyweds who had two children, a brand-new mortgage, and everything else that came with a ready-made family. The young couple was suffering from not only a lack of sleep, but apparently a lack of intimacy as well. He guessed it was his brotherly duty to help.

"Thanks! I owe you one." The smile plastered on Aiden's face reflected all of the wicked things he wanted to do to his blissfully ignorant wife. "When you find the right woman and settle down, I'll return the favor."

With that comment thrown out into the universe all willy-nilly, Koa's shoulders and back stiffened. He was perfectly content being a bachelor without anything or anyone to cause him drama. The last long-term relationship he was in ended with his clothes being thrown out into the middle of the front yard during a monsoon.

"Fine," Koa smirked as he shook his head. "Like that's gonna happen. I like being a bachelor, surfing when I want. Accepting any mission that I want. Dating whoever I want."

He smiled again when his brother-in-law stared at him with confusion, so he clarified.

"I'm living the life man," Koa beamed. "I'm living the life."

"Sure, whatever," Aiden responded flatly, ignoring the sympathetic tone in the other man's voice.

The other naval officer could only glare at him.

"Yeah, a whole weekend with the wife," Aiden added, rubbing his hands together like some maniacal villain.

"Stop! Damn it! I'm itchy, *again*." Koa smacked Aiden on the shoulder, hard.

Aiden was just about to retaliate with a punch to his brother-in-law's gut when a high-pitched, feminine voice called out to them from across the quad.

"Lieutenant Kaplan, please wait!" the senior officer beckoned as she hastily strode toward them.

Unable to stop them, Koa's eyes lit up and his ball-sack immediately tightened painfully.

"Who the hell is that?" he inquired, elbowing Aiden discreetly.

Needless to say, the petite, chestnut-haired beauty currently striding toward them, dressed in the standard Navy service uniform, was gorgeous. Her hair was up in a low, tight, bun, and her luscious curves even covered, left plenty to the imagination. However, there was no way to miss the unmistakable *F-off* look plastered to her otherwise lovely features.

"That's Commander Adrienne Mathis," Aiden casually informed. "She's my commanding officer, just transferred in from the base in American Samoa."

"And she's your *C.O.*" It wasn't a question.

"Yeah, you big chauvinist," Aiden frowned.

"Lieutenant Kaplan." Adrienne gave Aiden a pointed stare, completely ignoring the man standing to her side, raking her from head to toe then back again.

Aiden and Koa saluted respectfully, which she gracefully returned.

"At ease," she stated stiffly.

"Hello, Ma'am," Aiden greeted pleasantly and then returned to a more casual stance. "How can I help you?"

"I need you to look over these requisitions for next week's meeting," the woman replied, still ignoring the man she did not know.

"Ma'am, yes Ma'am," Aiden nodded. "I'll have my assistant pull the appropriate inventory sheets as well, Commander."

"Excellent." Commander Mathis still hadn't looked in Koa's direction. Causing him to unsubtly cough and clear his throat as he tried to get Aiden's attention, so he could be properly introduced to the exquisite creature currently disregarding him.

"Ma'am, by the way," Aiden continued nonchalantly. "This is Lieutenant Commander Koa Kapahu, my brother-in-law."

Finally, she turned to face him directly.

"Nice to meet you, Lieutenant Commander Kapahu," she replied with a tedious tone to Koa's massive chest instead of his face.

Now that she was standing only a couple of feet in front of them, Koa realized she was even more attractive up close. Smooth peanut butter complexion, in startling contrast to her green feline-shaped eyes, and cute button nose all nestled in a perfectly charming round face. Koa had never seen a woman with this combination of physical attributes and immediately deduced she was mixed-race, but whatever mixture she was took his breath away. And he couldn't help imagining what she looked like under her service uniform.

"You too, Ma'am." Koa gave her his patented *'melt-a-woman's-body-into-hot-molten-lust'* smile, which this particular woman, clearly blind, pointedly ignored, then turned back to Aiden.

Exasperated, she glanced at her watch, grimacing in the process.

"I'm late," she frowned, and adjusted her satchel more securely over her shoulder. "Lieutenant, I'll see you tomorrow morning in my office, O-eight hundred, for the debriefing."

"Yes Ma'am," Aiden acknowledged. "Have a good evening, Commander Mathis."

"Thank you," she nodded. "Lieutenant Commander Kapahu."

"Ma'am." Koa saluted, smiled, nodded back, and was extremely shocked when she turned, and without a backwards glance or flirtatious smile, made her way toward the designated officers' parking lot.

Stunned, Koa let out a low whistle.

"Damn!" he grimaced. "That woman should be the poster girl for how to lodge a stick up your ass."

"Nah, she's not that bad," Aiden chuckled. "She can be funny. Maybe not exactly *funny*, but I've seen her crack a smile, once. Or it might have been a snarl. I'm not sure."

Koa shook his head. Even though the woman was clearly a knock-out, he didn't have the time or the patience to break her in. Plus, she clearly outranked him, and fraternizing with a higher-ranking officer was a military taboo.

Too bad.

"C'mon, brah," he chuckled, diverting his mind and libido from the obviously uninterested female. "Let's go talk my sister into relinquishing the two rug-rats to my care this weekend. 'Cause after seeing who you have to deal with all day, you clearly deserve some, you know."

"Sex," Aiden clarified, wagging his brows.

"Would you please just stop saying that word?" Koa groaned through clenched teeth. "Great! Now I'm itchy. Again!"

SEALING THE DEAL

The drive to the subdivision where his sister and Aiden lived was a pleasant one. Thankfully, it was a beautiful sunny Hawaiian day with nothing but blue skies and a few puffy white clouds. Overhead, a flock of pelicans darted across the wide expanse on their way to catch an early dinner. That image made him want to go fishing and then and there he decided that was what he'd do.

After he dropped his brother-in-law home, that is.

The naval engineer and his sister had met in college in southern California and had become best friends during freshman year. Somewhere along the course of four years, the two fell in love, unbeknownst to each other, of course. Until a night of passion on graduation night produced a son that Aiden had never known of, until he reconnected with Kai six years later.

Soon after, they got married, had another kid, and now lived happily ever after.

"Aiden?" Koa gently tapped his sleeping passenger. "We're here."

A loud series of snores escaped the man's chest.

"Two more minutes," Aiden mumbled and readjusted on the seat, trying to get comfortable.

Koa could only smile.

Without hesitating, he punched the digital entry code to open the security gates then drove through, turning toward Aiden's street instead of in the opposite direction to his parents' house. Within a minute, they were parking in Aiden's driveway behind Kai's new minivan.

"Wake up," Koa grinned, unbuckling his seatbelt and opening his door. "You're not A.J., so I'm not carrying you inside, dude."

Slowly, Aiden retrieved his belongings and managed to get to the front door. With great effort he opened the door and quickly remembered to remove his shoes. Koa was already shoeless and closing the door behind him.

It was no surprise that Koa loved Aiden and Kai's home with its cathedral ceilings, winding staircase with intricately carved banister, bamboo flooring, and large palladium windows that let in tons of natural light. Aiden had surprised his new bride two weeks earlier with the extravagant wedding present. Looking around the half-decorated space Koa could still see unpacked boxes and misplaced furniture being stored in the formal living room. He made a mental note to take a weekend and help them get situated.

"Daddy's home!" Aiden announced loudly as he came into the house in the Kona Cove subdivision, located in Hawai'i Kai on the Southeastern side of Oahu, followed closely by his brother-in-law.

A.J., Aiden's five-year-old son was the first to greet him, launching his lithe little body into his father's awaiting arms.

"Hi, Daddy!" the energetic youngster bounced around like Disney's *Tigger*. "Dinner is almost ready."

"Is it?" Aiden tucked his son over his shoulder in a fireman's hold. "Where's Mommy?"

"She's upstairs with Aria, changing her diaper," A.J. gagged. "Yuck!"

SEALING THE DEAL

Aiden and Koa couldn't help their laughter at the little boy's disgust. A.J. loved his baby sister, but he definitely didn't like the smells that came along with her. Although, after she got a bath and was fresh and clean, he enjoyed playing with her and practicing reading her stories.

"Hey!" Koa exclaimed while taking his nephew from his dad's shoulder and tucking him under his arm like a human football. "Am I invited to dinner?"

"I guess so," his nephew giggled.

"You guess so," Koa snickered as he started to tickle him. "You guess so, you little *kolohe*."

As if on cue, Koa's sister, Kai came downstairs holding the newest member of the Kapahu-Kaplan household. Koa watched as his brother-in-law dropped his briefcase on the hardwood floor and strode toward his wife. The man's eyes practically glow with want and love.

It was all he could do not to toss his cookies.

Forgetting that anyone else was in the room, Aiden gently embraced both his wife and daughter, placing a sweet kiss on baby Aria's forehead before sealing his mouth over Kai's, and kissing the living daylights out of her.

"Mmm," Kai moaned into her husband's mouth making Koa feel ill. "That was very nice."

"Was it now," Aiden chuckled. "Maybe later we can—"

"Please stop. There are children present. Can we eat dinner before I never feel the urge to eat again?" Koa made an obnoxious face. "I'm starving."

Dinner looked and smelled delicious: teriyaki beef, steamed white rice, broccoli, and pineapple iced tea to drink, all from scratch. Koa had to admit his sister was a great cook, almost as good as their mom. He could cook as well. His parents taught both of their children to be self-sufficient and responsible at a very young age, and during the weekends and summers growing up he and Kai worked on the family's food trucks. He could make everything from a ham and cheese omelet to a full traditional Hawaiian luau feast, but these days he would rather eat out than go to a lot of trouble making fancy dinners for one.

Kai handed her brother the bowl of rice, interrupting his musings.

"So big brah," she began. "What are you and my husband up to?"

"Why we gotta be up to something?" Koa probed, voice sounding shaky and with a tad more of a Hawaiian lilt, even to his own ears.

Seeming just as guilty, Aiden looked up briefly, still spooning the rich beef and sauce over his rice.

"What makes you think we're up to something?" Aiden blustered, only further cementing his wife's suspicions.

Kai's brow arched as she glanced in her husband's direction, then Koa's, and then back to Aiden.

"Well," she replied, matter-of-factly tapping her bottom lip as if in deep thought. "There's your past track record, and your sixth sense for getting into trouble when you're together."

"It was your husband's idea to steal that pineapple," Koa explained.

"Wait a minute," Aiden rested his fork down on his plate. "If I recall, it was a certain Navy SEAL who hinted that I was a pus— a wimp if I didn't go into that pineapple field and *'borrow'* one of those overly-ripened fruit."

Playing along, Koa shook his head.

"Pardon me. I only *'suggested'* he do that. Is it my fault your husband can't say no to peer pressure," he clarified.

The Hawaiian man fell into his plate when Aiden hit him on the back of his head almost making him inhale a nose full of rice grains. Kai frowned at both of them, making him feel like the younger sibling.

"Spill it, now," the beautiful, amber-eyed woman commanded.

"Aiden wants me to take the kids this weekend, so you and he can... *light your fire...* so to speak," Koa blurted, feeling the food in his stomach begin to churn. "I said I would, if you agreed."

Koa, Aiden, and A.J. stared at her like she was a possible landmine leftover from World War II, holding their collective breaths as she contemplated their request. After several tense moments, she sighed.

"I suppose that would be good, having some time for myself," she agreed looking at her husband wryly. "Do you remember how to take care of a baby, Koa?"

"Of course, it's like riding a bike," he grinned. "Once you do it, you never forget."

"You're gonna change Aria's diapers and everything?" A.J. made a face.

All three looked over at Aria, who resembled a tiny, tanned angel, sporting a head full of black waves, eyes tightly closed, nestled securely in her bouncer.

"Yup, who do you think changed your diapers?" Koa reminded, making his nephew blush.

"Eww!" A.J. squealed before he laughed his head off, causing everyone at the table to join him.

In a cheerful mood, they returned to their dinners, chatting about Koa and Aiden's day on base, and Kai's current life as a stay-at-home-mom. She loved being a physical therapist, and she definitely missed her friends and coworkers at the naval hospital, but she wouldn't give up the opportunity to spend this precious time with her young family.

"I introduced Koa to Commander Mathis today," Aiden divulged as he took another helping of everything.

"How did that go?" Kai asked as she turned in her sibling's direction.

"Well, let's just say your brother has finally met a woman who can resist his *charm*, and he doesn't like it. Not at all." Aiden chuckled under his breath. "I personally think it's hilarious."

"So, '*Mr.-God's-gift-to-the-opposite-sex*'," Kai teased. "Commander Mathis didn't fall at your extra-large feet and beg to be your sex-bot?"

"No, she did not," he snorted. "She's not my type anyway."

"She's not?" Aiden's eyes bulged out a bit. "She's a beautiful, intelligent, no-nonsense, career-minded woman. What's not to like?"

Kai shot her husband a quizzical glare.

"But she doesn't hold a candle to you my lovely Hawaiian blossom."

"Uh huh," Kai snorted in a very loud very unladylike way. "You're not interested in her. Right, Koa?"

"She's *babelicious* and all, but that's about it," he clarified.

"So, if she gave you any encouragement at all, you still wouldn't be interested?"

Kai sat straighter in her chair, obviously interested in her brother's answer.

"Nah," Koa added. "She seems like one of those high-maintenance women. Always wanting to be in charge, boss people around, always getting her own way—"

The boisterous Navy frogman stopped when he noticed both adults sitting at the dining table watching him with eyes the size of saucers.

"What?" He wiped his mouth with his paper napkin. "Is something on my face?"

"Hmm," was the only sound his sister made before going back to her now lukewarm dinner.

CHAPTER TWO

"A.J.!" Koa yelled to his nephew, who looked like a younger, and tanner, mini replica of Aiden. "Don't go too close to the water, brah!"

"Okay, Uncle Koa!" the little boy yelled back while continuing to dig a deep hole near the shoreline, then using a plastic, orange beach pail to fill it with seawater.

Koa tugged on the legs of the beach canopy making sure it was still secure in the soft sand. He had taken their little group to a lesser-known beach on the windward side of the island, where he lived called Lanikai Beach. It was the perfect spot nestled in a quiet, residential neighborhood of Kailua.

The beach was a paradise in itself with sparkling white sand, and calm waters. For those needing to be more active, two uninhabited islands called the *Mokuluas or Moks* that served as a bird sanctuary could be reached via kayak. It was his favorite way to relax when not on a mission or in special training, lying on the soft Hawaiian sand, soaking up the temperate sunshine, and listening to quarreling seagulls overhead.

The dedicated officer knew that early January in Hawai'i was sheer perfection and today was no exception. However, today he had his two favorite people with him enjoying his sanctuary.

Lazily, he stretched his arms above his head to admire the serene cerulean blue sky dotted with billowy cotton-like clouds, drifting on the hibiscus-scented breeze. In the distance, festively painted sailboats caressed the Polynesian horizon. It was more like a Hollywood movie set than an actual place.

"Uncle Koa!" A.J. shouted, almost waking the sleeping bundle beside him. "I found a hermit crab!"

The little tyke held up the small crustacean by the shell.

"Cool, but put it down," his uncle suggested. "Gently, so it doesn't get hurt."

"No worries," A.J. stated, smiling sincerely, and did what he was told.

Startled by the unexpected noise, Aria began to fuss. At her loud complaint, Koa picked her up to feed her the pumped breast milk Kai had given him. He wasn't at all surprised when his tiny niece drank every last drop.

Afterward, he patted her back, and received two very loud, but satisfying burps. All that was left to do was hold her in his massive arms and sing to her, a Hawaiian Christmas song he'd remembered from his youth. Her uncle was ecstatic when his niece graced him with a toothless smile.

Or was it gas?

He changed her diaper, just in case, and placed her back into her carrier seat before glancing back up at A.J., who was talking and showing his newly dug watering hole and hermit crab to a very short, very curvaceous woman.

Quickly he grabbed Aria, who was now fast asleep, and began walking toward his nephew and the unknown female. From behind, the woman was a force to be reckoned with, with long legs, a nipped-in waist, and a full, firm round ass that made him want to fall to his knees and give God the glory for such a magnificent creation. Even wearing a conservative black, one-piece bathing suit with a sheer black sarong tied securely to her very tempting hips, she was a goddess.

As he neared, he caught the tail end of their conversation.

"… and that's where the hermit crab sleeps." A.J. confidently explained.

"Wow!" the woman exclaimed with a soft, French accent, much to the delight of his nephew. "I didn't know their shells were so important."

"When the crab gets bigger, he'll find a bigger shell."

"That's amazing!"

Koa could hear the smile in the woman's voice.

"Uh hum," he cleared his throat. "A.J., who's your friend—"

The woman turned to face him, and he immediately lost his smile.

"It's nice to see you again, Lieutenant Commander Kapahu."

"You too, Ma'am." He glanced between Commander Mathis and A.J.

She shook her long, wavy, chestnut locks.

"We're off duty and it's the weekend. Please, call me Adrienne."

"Ok… *Adrienne*." He suddenly felt nervous; palms starting to sweat. "I will as long as you call me Koa."

"Will do... *Koa*," she answered, her voice raspier than he remembered.

"So, I take it you two already know each other?" He nodded at his nephew who was looking up at them with those innocent grayish-blue eyes.

"These are Lieutenant Kaplan's children, aren't they?" Adrienne's cat-like, green eyes scanned the beach for their parents.

"Yes, these are Aiden's kids," he nervously explained. "This is my nephew, A.J., and my niece, Aria. Aiden's my brother-in-law."

"I see," the senior officer cleared her throat. "I met your sister, Kai, at the beginning of the week. She's lovely."

"Thanks, she's alright," he teased playfully, having difficulty looking away from the rounded cleavage peeking up over the neckline of her bathing suit.

Adrienne shook her head.

"I'm sorry," she apologized, cheeks tinted pink. "I haven't been at Pearl-Hickam very long. It's only been about a week or so. I didn't realize you two were related until yesterday."

As he continued to study her, the tip of the Commander's pink tongue darted out to play with the crease of her mouth, looking more sinful than was humanly possible. Koa shook his head trying to exorcise the baser instinct to grab her, rip off that annoying suit and plunge his cock deep into her sex.

"Koa?"

She was saying something, but for the life of him his brain wasn't processing it.

"Koa, are you okay? You look overheated."

"Do I?"

"Yeah, did you put on sunscreen?" she questioned with concern.

"Yeah." He chuckled.

Then he tried to relax, but his cock was getting harder the longer they spoke, and he was terrified she would notice the tenting of his swimming trunks.

"Could you do me a huge favor?"

She nodded yes.

"Could you watch Aria and A.J. while I take a quick swim?" Koa begged, needing to get away from the tempting minx. "I'd really appreciate it."

"Sure." Adrienne grinned at the sleeping baby, her green gaze softening. "Take your time."

"Thanks." He handed her the carrier and ran toward the calm Pacific. The gentle waves lapped over his bare feet and calves, chilly and invigorating, as he hurtled his aroused body into the clear depths until he was submerged from the neck down. Unfortunately, the cooler temperature did nothing to ease his rock-hard state.

Fuck!

After ten minutes or so his member still hadn't returned to its natural condition. Leaving him no choice but to take things in his own hand, pun *definitely* intended.

Not wanting to draw attention to himself, he turned his back to the beach. There he stood staring out at the *Moks* and the calm Pacific, who silently chastised what he was about to do, but he had no other choice. His damn cock pulsed and ached and demanded release.

Instantly, a vision of Adrienne bombarded his mind, naked, writhing, and begging beneath him. Her slender hands palming each breast, fingers pinching the erect peaks.

"Fuck me, Koa! You know you want to," his vision taunted.

Holy shit! Even an imaginary Adrienne was enough to wreak havoc on his brain.

Unable to tolerate more torment, Koa drove his hands beneath the water and reached inside his swimming trunks, pulling the errant appendage free. Without hesitation, he wrapped his fingers around its steely length, allowing himself to imagine it was Commander Mathis's fingers handling his cock. A low moan escaped from his heaving chest as the thought urged him on.

He began pumping his shaft, root to tip, in a slow motion, all the while imagining fucking the living daylights out of the unsuspecting woman on the beach. Her body tensing as he thrust his thick hard cock into her tight dripping pussy in one hard thrust. And then she'd relax as he stroked her with long, wet glides, in and out, in and out. All the while sucking on her pebbled nipples.

"*Shit!*"

Koa quickened his motions, up, down, up, down. Over and over and over again until he felt that familiar tingling sensation start at the base of his spine. His balls tightened, and that explosion of molten liquid burst from the depths of his body into the awaiting ocean.

"Fuck me!" his groan like a prayer to heaven thanking the orgasm gods for a speedy release as his member immediately softened. Quickly, he tucked it back inside his trunks, and then took several deep soothing breaths, cleared his mind of lustful thoughts and returned to his awaiting family and Commander Mathis. Adrienne.

As he approached, trying not to look too guilty, Koa noticed the Commander studying his physique, so he made sure to flex his pecs, subtly stretched his highly muscled arms, and smiled in that way he knew made women swoon. To his satisfaction, Adrienne licked her lips. Her plump lower lip begging to be bitten and he was just the man to do the biting.

Yeah, she'd be riding him before the night was over.

"How were they?" Koa's breathless question rushed out when she smiled, a perfect white toothy smile, causing his member to reawaken.

Damn it all to hell!

The insufferable appendage would be the death of him.

"They were very well behaved," Adrienne stated sweetly. "A.J. and I ate a few of the peanut butter and jelly sandwiches that were in the basket. I hope that was alright?"

"Yeah, of course, that was okay."

"Aria has been asleep the entire time," she continued quite pleased with herself.

"Good," he blushed.

Looking around at the picture-perfect surroundings, Adrienne sighed.

"I'll never get used to seeing beaches like this. Magnificent!" she beamed. "Why did you choose this particular beach?"

Koa pointed at a well-maintained bungalow several yards away.

"See that house right next to the dunes?" he beamed with pride. "The one with the blue and white surfboard leaning against the wooden fence—"

"That's Uncle Koa's house," A.J. concluded.

At the news, her eyebrow arched, and eyes narrowed suspiciously.

"How can you afford a beachfront house on Lanikai Beach of all places? You on the take?" She chuckled, letting him know she was only joking. "Really, how can you afford such a nice place?"

"Actually, I inherited it from my Uncle Daniel when he moved into a bigger place farther up the beach. He bought it back in the day before the real estate market went to… *poop*." He glanced over at A.J. "It was a fixer upper. I've spent four years restoring it. It's pretty nice, if you wanna see it."

"What?"

Koa gave her a million-watt smile before clarifying.

"The kids will be going down for their naps soon. You and I can keep each other company," he offered playfully, waiting for her to swoon.

Unfortunately, the swooning never happened. Instead, Adrienne's eyes narrowed into intimidating slits, her mouth curling into a feral grin, and he felt his knees tremble.

"*Wow!*" she exclaimed sarcastically. "You're a piece of work. You know that?"

"Pardon me?" Koa couldn't hide his confusion.

"You are not God's gift to womankind, Lieutenant Commander Kapahu," she snarled, voice low and menacing.

"Bu-but—"

"And I'm positive," she continued. "That whatever is in your pants isn't worth all of the hype."

Completely embarrassed, he stood there, mouth slightly opened, eyes wide with shock.

"All I meant was—"

"I know *exactly* what you meant," she interrupted.

"I'm sorry for assuming," he blustered and blushed. "I just wanted to spend some time with you. Get to know each other better."

She glanced around uneasily.

"I don't think that would be appropriate." Adrienne stood to gather her multi-striped beach bag. "It was nice seeing you again A.J."

His nephew ran over and hugged her around the waist before running back toward his sand swimming pool.

"Bye Adrienne!" his nephew called over his shoulder.

Then she turned to him.

"I'll see you on base Sailor."

"See ya," Koa mumbled as he watched her speedwalk away, her perfect ass mocking him. As he stared after her, he actually thought he heard his cock groan in disbelief. The woman had an iron will and it confused and intrigued him.

Huh!

Adrienne could not believe she had run into the gorgeous Lieutenant Commander twice in two days. She had seen him several times around the base during the past week, admiring his handsome roguish features, body taut with thick muscles, and lean waist. He had a body that was made to make women's insides turn to liquid pools of lust. The man should come with a label on his backside stating, *"Contents HOT... Handle with caution!"*

Again, she felt heat creep through every orifice of her over-stimulated body.

Unfortunately, Koa Kapahu should also have another disclaimer as well, but this one should say, *"Heartbreaker! Keep all body parts securely fastened."* What she wouldn't do for a hazmat suit for her already broken heart.

Never again, she had made that promise to herself a year ago. No more good-looking men. They were nothing but trouble, but that hadn't stopped her nether regions from quivering with delight the first time he smiled at her on base. Or when she turned around at Lanikai Beach and saw him striding toward her like a hungry jungle cat wearing only black *Nike* swim trunks, carrying a baby carrier and looking even sexier with it. If that was even possible for him to look sexier than he already was.

Damn it! Adrienne, stop rambling you're starting to sound insane.

In record time, she made it back to her apartment near base, relieved she had not gotten pulled over by the police for speeding. Stepping inside the cool space calmed her nerves a bit, but not enough. Quickly, she jogged to the bathroom, kicking off her flip-flops, stripping her cover-up and bathing suit as she trekked across the living area, down the hallway, and into her brightly decorated bathroom. Without delay, she turned on the shower to the coldest setting possible and stepped into the spray.

The frigid water hit her over-heated skin, causing her to gasp, but it felt good. Adrienne moved under it, drenching her shoulder-length chestnut hair, then pushing away the strands from her face. An unwanted picture of the Lieutenant Commander walking out of the Pacific, body covered with rivulets and glistening under the Hawaiian sun, made her nipples tighten into aching beads.

Desperate for release, she slipped her hand between her thighs, seeking out her dripping wet sex. Immediately, she plunged two fingers inside, pressing the heel of her hand against her pulsing clit. Unfortunately, it still wasn't enough. She wanted the hunky Hawaiian but had to settle for *this* instead.

"I'm an independent woman," she growled at the falling water. "I can take care of this *madness* myself."

Adrienne closed her eyes imagining the way he would kiss her; his lips hard and demanding as he slipped his agile wet tongue into her mouth. At the same time, she pushed her fingers deeper and began a slow, but steady rhythm, pressing and circling her palm over her engorged bud. Pleasurable warmth spread through her core, soft and liquid, resembling the watery fingers caressing her skin.

She pictured his cock, hard and long and decorated with thick veins, curving upward toward his bellybutton. She imagined that slight curve thrusting into her drenched sex. Rubbing that spot inside her that would send her to the moon.

"Koa," she whispered on a breathless moan.

And then it was like he was right there, in the shower beside her, pushing her against the cold tile as he pumped his hard length into her sopping wet channel. In and out. In and out. Stroking the inner walls of her sex with smooth caressing strokes. A man who looked as good as he did was no doubt going to be a master. No. He'd be a sex professor!

"Oh, God! Oh, God!"

The imaginary man was everywhere, in her mouth, in her pussy, against her body. Lost in her fantasy, she increased her pace, every muscle in her body tensing with anticipation and then she was coming, all over her still pumping fingers. Her sex tightened, and liquid pleasure surged through her until she was shaking with the force of it.

It was mind-blowing, and it wasn't even the real thing. Closing her eyes, she sighed, wishing for the first time in over a year, that she had never made that rule about not dating hot men again.

Damn!

CHAPTER THREE

"So, how was it having the house as a kid-free zone for an entire two days?"

"Amazing! Incredible! Spectacular! Freaking awesome!" Aiden's eyes were back to their regular well-rested state. "I owe you one."

"No worries, braddah," Koa replied casually. "Did you, *you* know?"

Aiden grinned wickedly, licking his lips and rubbing his hand over his heart.

"Oh, yeah!" He winked. "Many, *many* times."

"I'm sorry I asked." The tough as nails military man felt the bile rising in his throat. "Is that why you guys missed the family cook-out this morning?"

Every Sunday like clockwork the entire Kapahu family got together for a beach brunch and volleyball tournament with lots of great food and fun.

"Let's just say we had quite a bit of *fun* here, if you know what I mean." Aiden waggled his brows suggestively.

"*Yuck!*" Koa grimaced at his brother-in-law's insinuation.

"Yuck, what?" Kai asked, placing a glass pitcher of pineapple juice on the large outdoor dining table on the lanai.

"Your husband does not understand the concept of TMI," Koa stated, glaring at Aiden's bewildered expression.

With that said, Aiden's dark brow arched.

"Can I help it if my wife gets me hot?" The man grabbed his wife's butt as she poured him a glass of juice. With heated cheeks, Kai batted away his hands in a half-hearted attempt to protect her *'asset'*.

"That's it, I'm leaving," Koa announced, holding his hands up in a gesture of surrender. "I don't want to see my baby sister being fondled. I have to draw the line somewhere."

"Uncle Koa, are you going to see Commander Mathis again?" A.J. asked from his position on the nearby hammock. "She's nice."

Kai and Aiden glanced over their shoulders at the retreating Sailor.

"You guys saw Commander Mathis?" Kai asked after several tense seconds. "When?"

"We ran into her when I took the kids to Lanikai Beach on Saturday."

"Are you trying to hide it from us?" Aiden's gray-blue eyes narrowed suspiciously.

"No," he lied. "I just forgot."

"That's not true, Uncle Koa." A.J. shook his head. "You said that you could never forget her."

"When did I say that?" Koa glared, nostrils flaring from embarrassment.

"When you were asleep," his nephew informed.

"What?" Koa's brow arched almost to his hairline.

"Last night you were talking in your sleep," the little boy clarified.

"What did Uncle Koa say?" Kai prodded her unsuspecting five-year-old informant, who was more than willing to sell out his uncle for a couple of chocolate macadamia nut cookies and a glass of milk.

"He said, *'Adrienne, you are so beautiful! I'll never forget you! Your breasts are so—'*"

"Okay, son," Aiden grimaced. "We get the picture."

Koa felt his face heat at his nephew's revealing facts. His sister was smirking while Aiden was waggling both brows like Groucho Marx, and A.J. went back to playing with his *Transformers* action figures.

He shook his head.

"You can't hold things I say in my sleep against me."

"It's all right if you like her," Aiden chuckled. "Commander Mathis is a very beautiful woman."

"But she's not interested in me," he frowned.

"How do you know that? Did you ask her out?" Kai poured herself a glass, before resting the pitcher back on the table.

Slowly, Koa trudged back to where they were sitting, taking the glass out of her hands and taking a long swallow.

"I... I asked her to come back with me to my place and keep me company while the kids were taking their naps."

"You *propositioned* her?" Kai shook her head in disbelief.

"It wasn't exactly a *'proposition'* per se."

Immediately, his sister's brow arched, making him nervous.

"So, what were you expecting to happen while she was keeping you *company*?"

"I don't know," he fibbed unsuccessfully. "Some kissing, maybe some touching—"

"Hmm," was the only sound his sister made.

"What?" he inquired, truly not understanding the implications of his invitation to the prickly Commander.

Aiden cleared his throat to get his attention.

"You basically said, *'Hey I don't need to ask you out or take you to dinner or get to know you in any way, shape, or fashion. But I would like you to come to my place while children are present and—*"

A.J. watched his father intently.

"Ease the pain in my shorts," the other man concluded.

"Oh," he ruminated on the feedback. "*Oh!* Oh Shit!"

"Houston, we have liftoff!"

SEALING THE DEAL

Aiden made a loud rocket-like sound and pretended that the imaginary rocket crashed and burned.

Damn it! He was totally fucked!

CHAPTER FOUR

Adrienne spotted the goliath of a man clear across the greens of Pearl Harbor-Hickam. His standard Navy uniform pristinely pressed right down to the razor-sharp seams of his trousers, dark mirrored sunglasses blocking the view of his smiling hazel eyes.

Damn it!

Why was she always attracting perverts? He was a gorgeous pervert, but a pervert, nonetheless. She couldn't help the frown that was now covering her entire face.

Turning sharply to avoid crossing paths, she inadvertently ran into another Sailor who glared down at her, surprise filling his brown eyes.

"Sorry, Ma'am," the man apologized. "I didn't see you."

He bent down to help her retrieve her briefcase, and their foreheads bumped accidentally.

"Ouch!" They both yelped simultaneously, rubbing at their own injured areas.

"For the love of—" Adrienne tried to stand, but a wave of dizziness washed over her.

"I'm so sorry, Commander... uh..."

"Mathis," she filled in as they both tried to right themselves.

"Did I hurt you, Ma'am?" Guilt echoed under his smooth island lilt.

"It's alright," Adrienne mumbled, "It was my fault. I wasn't looking where I was going."

Without being asked, the thoughtful man helped her up from her crouching position and handed her the brown patent leather briefcase.

"No worries, Ma'am," he reassured, his kind chocolate brown eyes gleaming under his glasses.

It was then she noticed he was a handsome man, no doubt about it. He had a kind smile and boyish charm, and somehow, he reminded her of her dashing Navy SEAL.

Wait!

Not *her* Navy SEAL, maybe someone else's Navy SEAL. He had better *not* be someone else's Navy SEAL.

Damn! Stop babbling. Pull it together, Adrienne. The man has you unhinged.

"I'm Lieutenant Paul Choy." The man saluted still holding her other hand in his.

"At ease, Sailor." She grinned realizing they were still connected.

"Lieutenant Choy!" Adrienne heard Koa's animalistic growl directly in front of her and the Sailor helping her. "Get your hands off her. Right the hell now!"

Lieutenant Choy looked calm, unfazed by the sneering 6'7" combat-ready Navy frogman, looking like he was ready to do some bodily harm.

"Lieutenant Commander," the other man responded, saluted respectfully then relaxed. "I accidentally knocked the Commander's briefcase out of her hand and was only helping her up. That's all."

"That's right, Lieutenant Commander Kapahu." Adrienne glared at the territorial figure trying to intimidate the lower-ranked officer unsuccessfully.

Choy must either have nerves of steel or must not have the sense of a fruit fly, and soon he might have the life cycle of one as well judging by the look on Koa's face. For some reason, that look really annoyed her.

"Back down, Sailor." She straightened, hands on her hips, eyes narrowed in what she hoped was an intimidating glare. "That's an order."

Remembering her rank, Koa immediately stiffened, stood at attention and saluted.

"Ma'am, yes Ma'am, no disrespect intended," the SEAL explained. "Just thought you were being *'man-handled'* by this... by Lieutenant Choy."

Adrienne felt her cheeks heat at the insinuation she needed a knight in shining armor to protect her from anything, or anyone.

"I can assure you, Lieutenant Commander Kapahu, I can look after myself quite sufficiently—"

"Ma'am, yes Ma'am," Koa cut her off which made her anger rise even more. "I only wanted to help—"

"Don't say another word," she hissed through clenched teeth. "Or I'll have you written up for insubordination… harassment… and… *and* just being a gigantic pain in the butt."

Suddenly, she turned to Lieutenant Choy.

"Thank you so much, Choy," she gave a friendly smile. "Next time, I'll pay attention to where I'm going."

Koa stiffened, his hazel eyes staring at her like she was a caged lioness.

"Commander, I meant no disrespect," Koa huffed.

She shook her head vehemently, gripped the handle of her briefcase as if it were her only lifeline to keeping her temper in check.

"As for you, Lieutenant Commander Kapahu," she stated blankly. "If you come closer than fifty feet near me, I'll flay you where you stand. Got it?"

"Yes Ma'am." He saluted stiffly.

"Good!" Then as fast as her legs could carry her, she made a beeline back to the safety of her office and away from all these testosterone-filled men.

The day going smoothly, up until now, and secretly Koa hoped to run into the sexy woman he had been dreaming of all night. However, he was not expecting to completely stick his foot in his mouth or be humiliated in front of another officer.

"What the hell was that about?" Lieutenant Paul Choy, aka his cousin, glared at him as he stood staring after the retreating Commander. Mouth slightly opened, eyes narrowed, breathing like he had just run a very long, very cumbersome race. "Shit! Is she your woman?"

"No." Koa shook his head. "She is most definitely *not* my woman."

"Really," Paul snorted. "Are you sure about that?"

"Yes, I'm sure, asshole."

"Dude!" Paul scolded. "I'm not the one staring and drooling after her. Pull it together, son."

"Don't call me *son*," he countered with a scowl.

"Fine, *brah*." The other man snorted. "See ya later."

"Yeah." Koa's body lost its tension. "See ya."

Koa kept busy the rest of the day, trying unsuccessfully to rid his mind of the feisty petite Commander with the glorious ass. He trained with his men, doing underwater rescue dives and bomb location drills. Even worked out alone after training was finished for the day, but no amount of strenuous activity could distract him from her, and it seriously pissed him off. He'd never felt like this over a freaking woman. *Ever.* And he didn't want to, either.

When Koa finally left the gym, the sun had long ago set, sending long, ominous shadows across the naval base grounds. Quickly, he sprinted across the commons toward his black SUV when he realized he and only one other vehicle was still sitting in the officers' parking lot. Wanting to go home, he unlocked his vehicle, started it up, and almost made it out of his space before he saw a short, uniformed woman, skirt hitched up high on her toned peanut butter-colored thighs, trying to change a flat tire.

"Great! Freaking, great!" he mumbled under his breath.

Was the universe trying to mess with him? Did someone pin a *'Kick Me'* sign on his back when he wasn't paying attention?

Frustrated, he scrubbed a hand over his slightly stubbled chin contemplating if he should help her or if he should pretend not to see her. He sighed. Why did his parents drill it into his head to always lend a helpful hand to the fairer sex. Especially, when this particular member of the fairer sex would probably castrate him if he tried to help.

"Commander Mathis!" he yelled out of his open window. "Need some help?"

"I'm almost finished," She shook her head. "Go on. I've got it under control."

Koa snorted as he re-parked his SUV. The freaking woman was too stubborn for her own good, but for some unknown reason he liked it. Being a gentleman, he helped her to a standing position, before taking the tire iron from her grease-smudged hands.

"Come on, Ma'am," he stated confidently. "I've got it. Changing tires is one of my specialties."

"Really?" she grinned, letting down her guard.

"Yes." He blushed when she graced him with a rare full smile. He felt that little pain in his chest and grimaced.

Yeah, he was a goner.

In less than five minutes, he had her spare tire on and her deflated tire in the trunk. She looked relieved.

"Thank you so much, Lieutenant Commander."

"Since it's after hours, could we please use first names?" he teased mischievously.

She blushed, the simple act making his member flex.

"Sure, *Koa*."

"Great, *Adrienne*."

"Have a good night," the woman grinned as she dusted off her hands.

"You too."

He turned to get back into his SUV but was tapped on the shoulder.

"Koa?" The Commander stood ramrod straight. "Would you like to get some dinner? My treat."

The wheels in his head started turning, but he quickly shut them down. It was a kind gesture that she probably felt obligated to do. He didn't want her to feel bad, so he gladly accepted.

"Of course, I never turn down food." He grinned. "But there's one condition."

"What's that?" Her eyes narrowed and she braced for whatever lewd request the man was about to make.

"I'll pay."

"It was my suggestion, so I'll pay." She shook her head.

"Adrienne, Adrienne, Adrienne," he admonished, trying to hold back a chuckle. "I was raised to believe there are certain things a man must be able to do. Change a tire, open doors for ladies, cook, do yard work, be handy around the house, and—this is the most important item—pay for meals when accompanied by the fairer sex. And it's not a sexist thing because it was my mom who pounded it into my brain."

She hesitated for a moment, clearly reviewing his statement before reluctantly responding.

"Okay, you win," she beamed. "You can pay, this time. But the next time, if there is a next time, I'll pay. I'll just have to deal with your mom."

Koa raised his hands in surrender.

"I agree to your terms," Koa blushed. "But you'll be taking your life in your own hands."

"I'll remember that warning," Adrienne giggled. "Let's go! I'm starving."

What the Hell am I doing?

Adrienne sighed, gripping the steering wheel of her Camry with nervous hands. What was she doing having dinner with a man she had met only a few days ago? He was of a lower rank than her and she knew the rules. No fraternizing with anyone in uniform. Especially, one that could melt your panties with one charming smile, or some such nonsense.

Taking a quick glance around the small parking lot, she looked for his *Expedition*. The Hawaiian native gave her the address and said he'd meet her at the restaurant because he had to stop at a gas station. Headlights turning into the lot caught her attention, and she watched the now familiar SUV with the tinted windows take an empty spot several rows away.

Then an extremely tall, dark-haired man wearing a standard issue Navy service uniform emerged from the driver's side and she couldn't help but admire the way he carried himself; confident, sexy, and all man.

It was a truly awe-inspiring sight.

Bracing herself, she opened her door and climbed out, her legs a little shaky due to her nervousness. Immediately, he smiled when he saw her and waved before heading across the parking lot where she waited. As he strolled over, a barrage of naughty ideas bombarded her, making her blush. Thank goodness it was dark enough now that he couldn't see her guilty expression.

"Aloha!" he greeted casually. "Have you been waiting long?"

"No, just got here a few minutes ago. Traffic was still heavy." She grasped her purse strap to steady her hands as they made their way toward the restaurant's entrance.

"Yeah." His lopsided boy-next-door smile making her nipples harden. "Oahu is well known for being a bit congested. Once you get out of the touristy area, it's not so bad."

Koa held the door open for her, and she returned his shy smile as she walked past him into the busy establishment.

"I'll have to remember that." She smiled at how comfortable he always made her feel.

For dinner, they decided on this quiet little burger joint a few miles away from the base where they gorged themselves on bacon double cheeseburgers, hand-cut seasoned fries, and chocolate milkshakes.

"This is the best burger I've ever eaten," Adrienne told confidently. "How'd you find this place? It's so cute."

"A cousin of mine owns it with his wife," Koa gladly informed. "He opened it a couple of years ago. He's a classically trained chef, studied at the Culinary Institute of America and everything."

"Seriously?" Adrienne took another sip of her shake. "Why did he open a burger joint instead of a fancy restaurant?"

"Oahu has plenty of fancy restaurants," Koa informed with a shrug. "Keanu—that's my cuz— just wanted someplace relaxed where the locals could unwind and have a beer and good food. Also being near the base doesn't hurt his bottom-line financially."

Adrienne couldn't help admiring the man sitting across from her. His bright hazel eyes sparkling under the lights, a perfect smile lulling her into a calmness she hadn't felt in years, and it was driving her to distraction. All she wanted to do was dive across the Formica table, wrap her arms around his thick neck, and smash her lips against his.

Every time he licked his lips, Adrienne imagined she was his tongue.

Kill me now and take me out of my misery.

"Are you alright?" Koa asked; concern clouding his lovely irises.

My goodness! She loved the Hawaiian lilt to his voice that seemed to strengthen as he got more at ease.

"Yeah, it's been a long day." She anxiously cleared her throat.

"If you say so." He seemed to see past her forced self-assurance. "I'll pay the check and we can head out."

She nodded, unsure what else to do or say. When he returned, he left a generous tip on the tabletop before helping her up and out of her seat. I guess now she would have to go home.

Walking out of the diner behind her, Koa squinted until his eyes became accustomed to the dimly lit parking lot. Naturally, he took the opportunity to admire Adrienne's body. Unhurried, Koa's eyes traveled over her form watching the gentle swing of her lush hips as she glided forward. He loved her voluptuous figure. Not chubby, but not skinny, either. She was perfect.

The only other thing to distract him from her was the scrumptious aroma of chargrilled burgers and hand-cut French fries that hung in the air, tempting him to go back inside and get a couple more to go.

"I had a great time, Koa," she blushed as she got into her beige Toyota *Camry*. "Thank you."

It was his turn to blush this time.

"No worries, it was my pleasure." He closed her door and waited for her to start it up before turning and walking to his *Expedition*.

"See you around, Lieutenant Commander." She mock saluted through her open window.

"Yeah, see ya," he grinned, and then a sudden panic flooded him, and he couldn't let her drive away.

Turning back around before she pulled out of the parking spot he apologized saying, "I'm sorry again for, you know, today at the base. I didn't mean to insult you."

"Apology accepted," she grinned. "I have a tendency to overreact sometimes. My grandmother always teases me about it."

He chuckled, watching her blush and loving the sight of it.

"Thanks for clearing that up," he replied with a broad smile, turning toward his vehicle. "Goodnight, Adrienne."

"Koa!" she yelled across the parking lot making him turn back. "Do you want to meet up for dinner tomorrow night? If you have other plans, I'll understand."

"Sure, dinner tomorrow night sounds great!" He grinned. "I'll meet you at the officer's parking lot at eighteen-hundred hours."

Adrienne smiled.

"Perfect! I'll see you then."

CHAPTER FIVE

"Another perfect date. I mean, I didn't mean it was a date, *date*, just friends. Not even friends more like *coworkers* getting together for a meal... *Jeez!* I'm sorry. I have a tendency to ramble."

"That's okay," the handsome Sailor chuckled. "I like it when you ramble. It's very sexy, like your smile."

"Is that your best pick-up line, Sailor?" Adrienne teased, feeling her nipples harden beneath her blouse and prayed he didn't notice the traitorous buds.

Koa's smile vanished.

"I mean... *Crap!* I'm not trying to hit on you, Ma'am. I mean *Adrienne*. I only meant that you have a nice smile... with all your own teeth I assume... *Shit!* I didn't mean to imply you didn't have all of your original teeth. Please excuse me while I remove this shoe from my very large mouth."

Koa grimaced and wished a sinkhole would open up beneath his feet and swallow him whole.

Adrienne couldn't help the peal of laughter that escaped her chest.

"I'm sorry," she apologized with a grin. "I didn't mean to laugh, but I think my rambling is contagious."

Koa laughed too, a deep baritone sound that made her panties dampen and her hands begin to tremble.

"I think it is."

"Great choice in restaurants by the way." She removed her car keys from her purse and held them nervously in her sweaty palm. "I didn't picture a big guy like you enjoying sushi."

"Really?"

"Yeah, you look more like a meat and potatoes kind of man."

"I like that too," he replied, swallowing his last tempura-battered shrimp. "I'm a food connoisseur. I like almost everything, except liver. I *hate* liver."

He made a disgusted face at the thought of the item.

"I'm surprised that you ate almost as much as me," he complimented with a smirk.

"I love food too." She giggled. "I try to work out at least an hour every day, so I can eat whatever I want."

"Good to know" Koa chuckled. "I hate when a woman orders the healthiest thing on the menu then only eats half of it. Drives me bananas."

Their dinner was turning out to be the most fun and enlightening three hours of her entire life. Not only was Koa intelligent and could converse about anything and everything from world politics to the next winners of *Dancing with The Stars*, but he had a wicked sense of humor and always made her laugh.

"So why did you join the Navy and then the SEALS?" she queried, fascinated by the man sitting across from her.

"Well, I got a full ride to the University of Hawai'i right out of high school," he stated proudly.

"Lemme guess," she tapped her bottom lip with mock thoughtfulness. "Sports scholarship."

He blushed.

"Yes, I got a football scholarship," he admitted with a hearty chuckle. "But I was also an A student, honors classes, National Honor Society geek, Mathlete and everything."

"Impressive," she stated, surprised at his revelation.

"I got a degree in criminal justice," Koa continued. "But when it was time to join the police department it just didn't feel right. A buddy of mine was a junior officer in the Navy and got to travel and serve his country. I don't know why, but that sounded like something I'd be proud to do. It also helped that my father is ex-Navy. He was an engineer like Aiden and you."

"What made you decide to join the SEALS?" she prodded, wanting to know everything about him. "It's a dangerous position, to say the least."

"It is," he agreed. "No doubt about that, but I like the thrill of it—"

"You're one of those adrenaline junkies," she grimaced.

Without hesitation, Koa shook his head.

"No, when I'm not training or on a mission, I like the quiet life: being with my family, surfing, hanging out on the beach and seeing movies. It's sad to say, but those are all very *non-adrenaline-junky-things*." He winked, the simple gesture making her heart ache.

"Good to know," she replied, surprised at his answer.

"What about you Commander Adrienne Mathis?" Koa turned the conversation over to his beautiful companion. "Why did you join the Navy?"

"My dad was in the Navy also." She couldn't help smiling at the thought of her father. "He wasn't an officer or anything, just a regular seaman. He was a cook. A really terrific one too."

"Can you cook?" he asked, playful hazel eyes sparkling under the overhead pendant lights, the perfectly formed orbs resembling tiny jewels.

"Me?" she smirked. "I burn water."

He laughed a deep baritone that made her weak in the knees.

Dinner quickly flew by while she told him about life on base in American Samoa and several of the other bases she had been stationed at during her eleven-year Navy career.

In turn, he told her about his crazy family, extended and biological, and he smiled every time he mentioned their weekly Sunday beach volleyball game, surfing competitions that he frequented when not on duty, and his nephew and niece who he adored beyond words. She couldn't help but grin at his gentle nature. Especially, for such a mountain of a man, he was simply adorable.

"So," he sighed. "Now you know practically everything about me."

Koa chuckled as they walked to her car, the parking lot practically empty at nine on a Wednesday night.

"Who knew one night of prying you with sushi and tempura could unveil all of your secrets." She smirked.

"I think it's because you're so down-to-earth that I just feel I can tell you anything."

He gazed longingly at her, then some unknown emotion marred his eyes and then it was gone as quickly as it had appeared.

"Have a good night, Adrienne. It's been fun as always."

Then he bent and placed a quick, chaste kiss on her slightly flushed cheek, and she felt warmth engulf her entire body. When he pulled away, she instinctively grabbed him around his neck and brushed her lips against his.

It was just as she had imagined. His lips were full, soft and delicious.

"Mmm," he groaned making a gush of moisture pool at her sex. "Adrienne, you're gonna make me do something that I've been trying not to—"

"Please. Just kiss me, Koa," she pleaded, unashamed of the longing the Hawaiian demigod evoked in her. "Kiss me, just once."

And he did! Boy, did he ever! He kissed the *bah-Jesus* out of her!

Caught up in the moment, his body relaxed as he lifted her with ease and sat her on the hood of her vehicle, then settled between the vee of her thighs, bringing his rock-hard erection directly against her now throbbing sex. Instinctively, he angled her head to get a better seal over her lips. All the while, his talented tongue persuaded her to give him entrance. Once inside, Koa plunged into her mouth in a soft, slow glide, exploring every nook and cranny of the warm space, their tongues sliding erotically against each other in a fierce mating dance.

Adrienne moaned into his mouth unable to hold it inside any longer.

"Mmm," she hummed against his lips. "You're a really good kisser."

Koa pulled away long enough to say, "I've wanted to do this since the first time I saw you on base talking to Aiden."

"You did?" Her breathing coming in short choppy pants.

"Absolutely," he answered as he nipped her collarbone causing her to yelp then quickly soothed the slight sting with his tongue. "I need to feel you. All of you, Adrienne."

Out of her mind with lust, she battled the need to consume every virile inch of him, right on top of her car for all of Oahu to see.

"I don't think that's a good idea, Lieutenant Commander."

He chuckled.

"I love it when you call me by my title."

His rather large hand fondled her left breast over her blouse driving her to distraction.

"Grr!" he growled. "Your nipple is so damn hard."

Then he pinched the aching peak between his thumb and forefinger, the movement making her gasp loudly.

"I c-can't have s-sex with you!" she tried to explain through the lust-hazed cloud descending on her. "We hardly know each other!"

Koa shook his head.

"We don't have to have sex."

He sounded as desperate as she did and that eased her tension.

"Do you trust me?" he questioned with pleading eyes.

"Yes," she answered without hesitation.

"Then let me make you feel good, Adrienne." He pinched her nipple again.

"Okay," she stiffened. "But not on top of the car."

He nodded while picking her up like she weighed nothing at all, walked to his Expedition, unlocked it, and placed her gently on the backseat before sliding onto the seat beside her.

"We won't do anything you don't want to," Koa promised, and she believed him.

Gently, he lifted her chin, so they were looking directly at each other—hazel to green.

"I promise no clothes even have to be removed," he explained to the wide-eyed goddess beside him, nervously biting her bottom lip. "Okay?"

She swallowed, hard.

"Okay," she moaned, unable to stop the tortured sound from escaping. "But won't someone see us?"

He shook his head.

"My windows have a very dark tint," he reassured. "At night, you can't see inside unless the light is on."

"Good to know," she grinned.

Without another word Koa went to work, unbuttoning her shirt to the waist, but leaving it on and still tucked into her trousers. With deft fingers he unsnapped the front clasp of her bra releasing her breasts from their lacey prison.

"Holy shit!" he whispered. "Your breasts are even more perfect than I imagined. They are so soft and full and perky."

Then his lips sealed around one tight nipple sucking and licking it with an expert tongue and then released it with a wet pop to give the same attention to the other one. The ministrations making her cream her already damp cotton panties.

"Koa," she moaned, her voice low and raspy like she'd just woken up. "I need *more*."

He nodded, slipping his hand down to the button of her pants and undoing it one-handed. Adrienne didn't even want to imagine how he learned to do that little trick. All she knew was that she needed him, and she needed him right now.

Slowly, Koa unzipped her pants, the sound even louder in the confines of the SUV.

"I'm gonna fuck your sweet little pussy with my fingers. Is that okay?"

She nodded her consent.

"Open your legs, kitten. Yeah, just like that. Such a good little Commander," he chuckled arrogantly making her even crazier for him. On a mission, his fingers found their way beneath her trousers.

"Hurry!" she commanded through the fog of lust he was creating.

"I've been dreaming about this for a long time, kitten."

She frowned at his new endearment for her.

"Don't call me that."

"What?"

"*Kitten*," she sighed, enjoying his calloused palm against her heated skin. "It sounds so… *naughty*."

"It's meant to," he chuckled.

"Can't you call me something less *pet-like*?"

"No can do." He laughed, his voice sounding raspier than usual.

With ease he slipped his hand inside the cotton material barring his entry, past her panties as he slowly began to stroke the soft curls of her mound, and then quickly found her slick entrance.

"You are so damn beautiful. Do you know that, Adrienne?"

She nodded.

"Well, you are... *Damn beautiful.*"

"Koa," she moaned. "Please."

Desperate to hear her come, he looked directly into her half-closed eyes and growled.

"Please what, kitten?"

"Please, touch me."

At her request, he swiftly plunged one thick digit into her tight wet channel. Adrienne gasped at the invasion.

"Kitten," he hissed through clenched teeth. "You are so freaking wet for me. I can't wait until it's my cock in this tight heat instead of my finger."

Slowly, he pumped that finger, in and out, in and out, driving her insane with lust, then he added another finger never stopping that incessant pumping. When those were gliding into her easily, he surprised her by adding a third.

"Shit!" she yelled, as she pushed against his hand, seeking more, wanting more, *needing* more.

"Am I hurting you?" Koa stilled his motions.

"No." She started humping his drenched fingers. "Don't stop! Please don't stop! I'm so close!"

Koa quickened his movements; finger-fucking her with almost inhuman speed, watching her intently as she moved against him.

When he realized just how close she was teetering on the edge of release, he used his thumb to circle her pulsing clitoris.

The motion caused her to see nonexistent stars.

"Just like... *that*... *I'm gonna come!*"

"Open your eyes," he commanded, his voice hoarse with need. "I want to see you."

He leaned down and sucked one dark nipple into his mouth, lavishing the hard peak with long wet licks.

It was all it took to send her body over the cliff and slamming it into the most toe-curling orgasm she had ever experienced.

When her breathing slowed, Koa leaned over and kissed her gently.

"That was perfect, kitten." He smiled at her even though his features were strained with the need for his own release.

"What about your situation?" Adrienne stared down at the gigantic bulge tenting his pants.

"We'll save it for next time." He chuckled.

"It's not really fair, is it?" she commented, feeling guilty.

Sweetly, he kissed her on the forehead.

"If I touch you again," Koa warned with an impish grin. "I won't be leaving this vehicle without fucking you within an inch of your sanity."

She giggled as he adjusted his erection before quickly re-snapping her bra, buttoning up her shirt, and refastening her pants.

The thoughtful actions made her heart tighten in her chest.

"There," he winked. "Back to normal, Commander Mathis."

"Thank you, Lieutenant Commander Kapahu." She laughed.

"Now," he sighed. "We've gotta get going or we might never leave this truck."

CHAPTER SIX

Three months later...

"I can't believe you haven't *SEALed* the deal yet. Get it? 'Cause you're a SEAL!" Paul Choy, cousin and royal pain in the ass taunted. "What the hell is taking so long? If I was dating Commander Mathis—"

"We are not dating," Koa lied, trying to eat his barbeque ribs, potato salad, and spicy grilled corn-on-the-cob in peace while his cousin drilled him like a convict on death row.

"Yeah," Paul continued. "If I was dating a hot babe like that, we'd be having hot, sweaty sex morning, noon, and several times at night. I'd wear that pussy out."

Koa punched him in the arm.

"Don't talk about her like that, *brah*."

Paul rubbed his arm.

"Sorry, didn't mean to offend you... or your... *whatever*. All I'm saying is what are you waiting for?" His cousin took a large forkful of potato salad and stuffed it in his mouth.

"She's a senior officer," Koa replied, as if that was the only explanation needed.

"So?"

"So," he rolled his eyes. "It's against protocol. You know, no fraternizing with a higher-ranking officer, blah, blah, blah."

"But she was the one who asked you out." Paul's eyebrow arched.

"Yeah," he scoffed.

"Well, consider it an order from another officer to go ahead and boff her brains out." His cousin pumped his hips suggestively making him want to punch him again.

"Adrienne wants to take things slowly," he explained as he took a bite of his delicious sticky-sweet ribs, licking the sauce off of his fingertips without shame. He loved his family's weekly Sunday beach brunch and volleyball tournament.

"Who wants to take what slowly?" Aiden asked, sitting beside them at the picnic table, holding Aria as she slept. His five-month-old niece looked more and more like his sister, except for those mesmerizing gray-blue eyes she inherited from her daddy.

One day he hoped to have beautiful children, ones with his skin complexion and big cat-like green eyes.

Shit! Where the hell did that thought come from?

Shaking the disturbing idea out of his mind, he took another bite of his food. Adrienne wouldn't even label him as her boyfriend; much less have babies with him. Although, he was positive their offspring would be breathtaking.

"Nothing, don't worry about it." Koa reached over and placed a quick kiss on his niece's forehead.

"Don't worry about what?" Kai joined the growing inquisition, and he wanted to bury himself in the sand until they all forgot about his lack of a love life.

He wasn't complaining. On the contrary, the past three months with Adrienne were some of the best months of his life. They ate dinner together at least twice a week. Went to the movies every Saturday and spoke on the phone every night like two teenagers. He had even brought her to his parents' house several times for dinner. Their relationship was smooth and comfortable, and he could picture them spending the next several decades doing the same thing.

That thought sometimes terrified him.

Everything was perfect, except for the lack of sexual intercourse. They'd kissed and did some messing around, but that was it. Adrienne wanted to take things slowly and he didn't want to scare her off. Especially after she had told him her last boyfriend cheated on her with her assistant and she had sworn off dating. No, he wouldn't rush her. He'd just keep taking long, cold showers no matter how high his water bill got.

"Nothing." His dick automatically stiffened at the thought of her, and he shifted on the seat to get more comfortable.

"Koa hasn't *SEALed* the deal with Adrienne yet," Paul joked, right before Kai pinched his arm hard. "*Ouch!* What was that for?"

"Pig!" she scolded; amber eyes glowing like a tigress. "Adrienne has every right to take things slowly. It's her body and her heart on the line. If Koa cares for her, he'll wait until she's ready."

His sister placed a kiss on his blushing cheek.

"Yeah," Aiden added. "But three months is a long time to wait."

Kai's brow arched almost to her hairline.

"Excuse me?" She cleared her throat dramatically. "You waited for four years for me."

"That was different." Aiden's face reddened.

"Why was it different?"

"It was different because… *because…*"

"I'm waiting." His wife tapped her fingers anxiously on the wooden tabletop.

"It was different because I secretly loved you: mind, body, and soul." Aiden grinned at his better half who only shook her head, her shoulder-length curls caressing her cheeks.

"You are so full of it," she snorted.

"Yes, my Hawaiian goddess." He pulled her toward him and devoured her lips with a passionate kiss. "I was full of love… *for you*… and only *you*. I just didn't know it then."

"That's the sweetest thing you've ever said to me," Kai gushed and sealed her lips to her husbands in another passionate union.

Paul shook his head.

"See, that's what I'm talking 'bout!" Their single cousin praised. "Aiden, you are the man! Can you teach me your moves, *Sensei?*"

Aiden grinned arrogantly.

"Sorry, son. You couldn't *handle* my moves."

"So, I was hoping you'd go with me to the officers' banquet this coming Saturday?" Koa's voice sounded shaky over the phone, and she didn't know if he was nervous or if they had a bad connection.

"I don't think that would be—"

"Let me guess," he paused dramatically. "Appropriate?"

"Correct."

"Are you ashamed of me?" he huffed and did not care if he sounded like a wuss.

"Of course not!" she bristled. "Not in the least."

"Then be my date for the banquet," he encouraged with a grin. "I'll even buy you a corsage."

He was just so charming.

"It wouldn't look right," Adrienne sighed. "A senior officer dating a—"

"Oh! I understand," he bristled this time, the sound hurting her heart. "You don't want to tarnish your image. I get it. I do."

Koa cleared his throat and waited for her response, but none came.

"I just want to make this clear," he continued. "I'm a college graduate. I own my own home. I make a decent wage and I'm loyal to a fault. I would never disrespect you by cheating and I'd cut my own arm off if I knew I'd caused you pain, but I'm not a lap dog."

"I never said that!" she gasped.

"You implied it," he countered. "Same thing."

"You're taking this way out of proportion, Koa."

"No, I don't think I am. I've been patient. I've tried to show you that I don't want you just for sex," he rambled and didn't care. "I mean I want to have sex with you. What man in his right mind wouldn't. Shit! I'm babbling. See what you do to me, kitten?"

"Koa," she pleaded. "Let's go separately and we can meet up afterwards for coffee."

"I don't drink coffee."

"You know what I mean," she huffed with exasperation. "Juice, a drink, water. I don't know."

A low growl could be heard over the telephone receiver.

"What do you consider me?" Koa pressed wanting to know where he stood.

"Excuse me?"

"Me," he clarified. "What am I to you?"

"You're my friend," the words rushed out of her. "My only true friend on the whole island."

"Got it," he grumbled, irritation filling his tone. "We're just *friends*."

"Yes," she held her breath.

"Will we ever be more than friends?"

"I'm not sure," she answered truthfully not wanting to lead him on.

There was a long pregnant silence before he responded.

"That's all I needed to hear. I'll see you at the banquet, Commander Mathis."

Then he hung up the phone.

"Koa!" she yelled into the receiver. "Koa, wait!"

Well damn!

She'd screwed up, big time, but it was true. She wasn't ready to date. Better to make that clear now than have him resent her later. It was all for the best.

Wasn't it?

The recreation center on base never looked better. The large rectangular room was elegantly decorated with crystal chandeliers, vases filled with fresh white roses and greenery, a large parquet dance floor, and round dining tables set to the nine. If he was not so miffed at Adrienne, he would be impressed, but sadly, all he wanted to do was go home and read a good book.

"Thank you for inviting me to the banquet, Koa."

"No worries, little cousin." Koa tried to smile at his younger cousin, Noelani, but couldn't.

"Why don't you go over there and talk to her?" the lovely young lady suggested, seeing how miserable he was.

"Nah," he said stubbornly. "She wants to be just friends."

The tall, dark-haired beauty who just graduated from the *Fashion Institute of America* rolled her eyes at him.

"So, you're just going to give up?" Noelani critiqued.

"Yeah, pretty much," he frowned.

"I never thought I'd see the day when the big bad Lieutenant Commander Koa Joseph Kapahu would fold like a house of cards."

"*What?*" he snapped. "I'm not folding."

"Whatever you say, buddy," she stated, taking another long sip of her white wine spritzer.

Dinner on base was catered by his aunt, a well-known chef and entrepreneur, and was delicious as usual, but for some reason he just wasn't hungry. He took a few bites of the roasted chicken with a buttery herbed crust and a couple of bites of the garlic flavored purple potatoes and asparagus with hollandaise sauce before pushing his plate away.

"If you're not going to finish that, can I have it?" Paul drooled over his empty plate.

"Go ahead. Here, help yourself." Koa traded his almost full plate for his cousin's empty one. "Why did you have to sit next to me?"

"Because I don't have a date and I didn't want to sit by myself." Paul took a forkful of potatoes and shoveled it into his mouth.

"You eat like a pig." Koa shook his head in disgust. "That is why you don't have a girlfriend."

"Apparently, you don't have one either," Paul mumbled under his breath, ignoring the low growl that escaped Koa's chest.

"Now, boys," Noelani chastised. "Behave. We don't want the military police to haul you two away to the brig, do we?"

"No, Ma'am," both men answered their cousin in unison.

As they were sitting around, mumbling, grumbling, and having a terrible time, Noelani grabbed her cousin's wrist.

"Koa, dance with me," she suddenly begged.

"I don't feel like it." He pouted and took a drink of his soda. "Ask Paul."

"No, way!" The sassy female shook her head. "He's got two left feet."

"I do not!" Paul whined loudly.

"Do too!" she poked.

"Do not!" Paul sneered.

"Do too!"

"Jesus, for all that is decent and holy!" He grabbed Noelani by the hand and hauled her to the dance floor. "I'll dance with you. Just please stop bickering like children. You're giving me a headache."

The young woman gave him a brilliant smile, showing off perfect teeth.

"Thank you, Koa," she purred, brushing up against him seductively.

Koa's eyes widened with shock.

"What the hell are you doing, Noelani?!" He stepped back to put more space between their bodies. "Are you drunk? No, you can't be drunk. You've only had one glass of wine."

"*Shh!*" she chastised. "You'll thank me tomorrow."

"What for?"

"You'll see," and with those words she placed a chaste kiss on his lips, causing him to growl.

"You remember we are *cousins,* right?" he grumbled through clenched teeth. "And we live in *Hawai'i*, not some backwoods place where people still marry their sister. And even if the entire human population was to die out, and we were the only two people left on Earth and it was our job to procreate, I still wouldn't."

Noelani pinched him, hard, but discreetly.

"I'm not coming on to you, you moron," she growled back, not even trying to mask her annoyance.

"Then, what are you doing?"

"Your girlfriend is watching us."

"She's not my girl… Hold on! She's watching us?"

"Yup," Noelani giggled. "She's been eyeing you like a side of beef at a vegan potluck from the moment we walked into the ballroom."

Koa scanned the room, finally finding his *'friend'* at the bar ordering a drink.

Adrienne looked gorgeous wearing a knee-length, form-fitting strapless emerald gown, hugging all those alluring curves. Conservative two-inch beige heels adorned her feet. Her makeup was simple: just eyeliner, mascara, and sheer lip gloss. Tonight, her thick chestnut hair hung in loose curls over her slender shoulders enhancing her green eyes.

Koa felt an unfamiliar ache in his chest and dismissed it as an air bubble.

"No, way!" He allowed his overly zealous cousin to pull him closer.

"Way!" She rolled her eyes. "Why do you think I grabbed your butt when we were at the bar? How obtuse can you be? That woman wants you, badly."

"Well, I know I have a nice pair of glutes—"

"Eww, yuck!" she squealed. "I think I just barfed in my mouth."

Unfazed, Koa laughed a good old belly shaking laugh as he twirled his obviously disgusted cousin around the crowded dance floor.

"Is she still looking at us?" he asked after a few more minutes. His curiosity was getting the better of him. He was hooked and he damn well knew it.

"Who?"

"Adrienne," he snorted.

"I don't know.," Noelani pouted. "I've been making puppy-eyes at that hot Sailor over by the far corner, near the band."

He glared at her, annoyance blanketing his features.

"Never mind."

Jeez! His meddling family members were gonna send him to the Looney bin.

Adrienne felt like she was on fire and not in a good way, as she watched the ruggedly handsome Lieutenant Commander in his dress whites being groped by a very pretty, very tall, elegant Hawaiian woman in a deep plum halter gown and matching four-inch heels. Which brought the Polynesian goddess almost to Koa's chin. The other woman wore her dark locks up in an elegant chignon, and her only makeup was eyeliner and lip gloss, and she still was breathtaking.

She grimaced. Well, it was her own fault. Telling the man of her dreams they were just friends, when the truth of the matter was, she wanted him more than she wanted her next fix of cookie-dough ice cream.

Another bout of jealousy slammed into her when Koa leaned down and whispered into the woman's ear. She could see her smiling from across the room and it was all she could do not to walk over and rip the bitch's hair out of her scalp.

Jeez!

She was so messed up. He wasn't hers to be jealous over.

Was he?

After ordering her second rum and *Coke*, Adrienne decided to leave the festivities, and go home to finish her half pint of *Ben & Jerry's Chunky Monkey*.

"Where are you going?" Kai asked as she and Aiden came to stand beside her.

Aiden in his dress uniform, looking like a GQ model, and Kai looking like a curvaceous supermodel in a raw silk, burgundy one-shoulder, full-length gown with strappy black pumps. Her ebony curls flat ironed straight and flowing in layers over her naturally toned shoulders. Kai's makeup was nothing more than lip gloss and eyeliner, but she didn't even need that to make her stand out. Being 5'8" and built like a brick house didn't hurt either.

"I'm not feeling well," she quickly lied.

"I'm sorry to hear that," Kai added, her lovely amber eyes narrowed suspiciously.

"Do you know who that woman is with your brother?"

Aiden tried to answer, but his wife nudged him with her elbow before answering.

"No, I've never seen her before."

"Aiden, do you know that woman with Koa?"

"Huh?" His gray-blue gaze sweeping around the room as if he were trying to avoid looking at her directly, so she cleared her throat trying to get him to focus.

"Do you know her?" she asked again.

Aiden glanced at his wife again.

"Uh… no… *no*… I do not."

"Well, I've had enough fun for one night." Adrienne felt a deep sinking feeling in the pit of her stomach. "I'm leaving now."

"Alright." Kai gave her a quick hug. "I hope you feel better."

"Thanks," she pouted, unable to stop herself. "See you on Monday, Aiden."

"See ya, Adrienne."

Aiden and Kai watched her leave.

"Kai?"

"Yes, my love?"

"Why didn't we tell Adrienne that the woman hanging all over your brother is your cousin?"

She grimaced. Well, it was her own fault. Telling the man of her dreams they were just friends, when the truth of the matter was, she wanted him more than she wanted her next fix of cookie-dough ice cream.

Another bout of jealousy slammed into her when Koa leaned down and whispered into the woman's ear. She could see her smiling from across the room and it was all she could do not to walk over and rip the bitch's hair out of her scalp.

Jeez!

She was so messed up. He wasn't hers to be jealous over.

Was he?

After ordering her second rum and *Coke*, Adrienne decided to leave the festivities, and go home to finish her half pint of *Ben & Jerry's Chunky Monkey*.

"Where are you going?" Kai asked as she and Aiden came to stand beside her.

Aiden in his dress uniform, looking like a GQ model, and Kai looking like a curvaceous supermodel in a raw silk, burgundy one-shoulder, full-length gown with strappy black pumps. Her ebony curls flat ironed straight and flowing in layers over her naturally toned shoulders. Kai's makeup was nothing more than lip gloss and eyeliner, but she didn't even need that to make her stand out. Being 5'8" and built like a brick house didn't hurt either.

"I'm not feeling well," she quickly lied.

"I'm sorry to hear that," Kai added, her lovely amber eyes narrowed suspiciously.

"Do you know who that woman is with your brother?"

Aiden tried to answer, but his wife nudged him with her elbow before answering.

"No, I've never seen her before."

"Aiden, do you know that woman with Koa?"

"Huh?" His gray-blue gaze sweeping around the room as if he were trying to avoid looking at her directly, so she cleared her throat trying to get him to focus.

"Do you know her?" she asked again.

Aiden glanced at his wife again.

"Uh... no... *no*... I do not."

"Well, I've had enough fun for one night." Adrienne felt a deep sinking feeling in the pit of her stomach. "I'm leaving now."

"Alright." Kai gave her a quick hug. "I hope you feel better."

"Thanks," she pouted, unable to stop herself. "See you on Monday, Aiden."

"See ya, Adrienne."

Aiden and Kai watched her leave.

"Kai?"

"Yes, my love?"

"Why didn't we tell Adrienne that the woman hanging all over your brother is your cousin?"

"Because." His wife snorted.

"Because, why?"

"Because Adrienne needs a swift kick in the ass when it comes to my brother and Noelani is the shoe. Get it?"

He shook his head.

"No… no I do not."

"Baby," she kissed the side of his mouth playfully. "Don't worry your pretty little head over it. I've got this covered."

I'm insane! I'm insane! I'm insane!

What was she doing standing in front of Koa's beach bungalow at… twenty-three hundred hours?

Yes, it was true! She had finally lost her mind.

The tall, gorgeous Navy officer with the perfect smile and the gentle mannerisms, made her crazy. In reality, she was miles passed crazy. She was downright desperate for him.

Steeling her nerves, she rang the doorbell, waited a few seconds then rang it again. Just as she was about to ring the damn thing for a third time, Koa's shadowy form appeared behind the decorative frosted-glass panel of the front door. She heard him swearing in Hawaiian before he jerked the door open.

"What the—?" he growled before realizing it was her. "It's you. What do you want, Commander Mathis?"

Shit! He used her full title. It probably wasn't a good sign.

Adrienne ogled him up and down regaling in his unadulterated masculinity, sleep-tussled dark hair, and drowsy hazel eyes. He was the epitome of male strength all wrapped in low hanging gray pajama bottoms and nothing else. She swallowed, hard, trying not to jump his bones right there on his doorstep.

Suddenly, she felt overdressed in her black t-shirt and denim Bermuda shorts. Koa didn't bother to check her out, which made her worry even more.

One brow rose, and she swore she heard him mutter a curse in Hawaiian.

"What do you want?" he repeated without a smile.

"Umm, I'm not sure," she answered as he stared at her with a look of disdain.

Tired, he rubbed his eyes then began closing the door in her face.

"Then come back when you are sure," he yawned without emotion. "I have training in the morning and need to get some sleep. Goodnight, Commander Mathis."

"Koa," she pleaded with desperation. "Please wait a minute."

"You've got one minute."

"I'm sorry."

"You're sorry for what?" he declared with a scowl. "Treating me like a castoff, not going to the banquet with me, for leading me on for the past three months? Go ahead, Commander. What exactly are you sorry about?"

She cleared her throat.

"For all of it!" she huffed. "I'm sorry for all of it."

"Thanks," he stated matter-of-factly. "Apology accepted."

She smiled, feeling the tension leave her body.

"Now, if you'll excuse me, Commander," Koa added. "I need to get my beauty sleep."

"Wait a second!" She felt her cheeks heating. "That's it?"

"Yeah, *friend*," he replied sharply. "I accept your apology and now I'm going back to sleep."

"Are we going to see each other anymore?" the panicking woman blurted. "Dinners and movies and stuff, volleyball and *whatever*?"

"I don't think so." Koa shut the door and Adrienne could see his shadow moving away from the entrance and farther into the dimly lit house.

Well, I'll be damned!

The arrogant asshat was *actually* going back to bed, leaving her alone to seethe on his front step. Alone and horny as hell.

No! No! No! That's not why she came. Was it?

Still in shock she banged on the door this time and several minutes later, Koa reopened the door.

"Why are you still here?" he sighed.

"You arrogant, selfish, Neanderthal of a *sonofabitch*!" she hissed loudly.

His sleepy hazel eyes widened.

"I'm a *sonofabitch*?" he exclaimed. "Lady, I've been more than nice to you. I've introduced you to my family. I've taken you out to dinners. I've been patient and all you've done is lead me on, and then you expect me to just fall at your—"

Koa's rant was stifled in midsentence by Adrienne jumping into his massive arms while sealing their mouths together in a passionate embrace. She was out of her mind with hot, dirty desire and she couldn't wait any longer to have his hard cock inside of her already dripping sex. Consequences be damned!

"Adrienne," he whispered, as he pulled away from her lip lock. "What are you doing?"

"Trying to seduce you," she wheezed.

"Really?" The carnal expression creeping across Koa's features wasn't comforting at all. He reminded her of a dog with a bone. "Then I guess you'd better come inside before the neighbors call the cops."

"Just hurry, Koa, before I spontaneously combust!" She informed with all seriousness.

The little lopsided slant to his full pouty lips sent a bolt of lightning through her inner core, heating her from the inside out.

He chuckled.

"We wouldn't want that now, would we?"

He kissed her back then suddenly stopped.

"Wait!" he gasped. "Do I need to go down the street and buy some condoms?"

"You don't have a stash here?"

"No," he replied. "I haven't had sex in eighteen months."

Her brows arched in disbelief.

"You're lying," she responded without heat.

He laughed, shaking his short cropped ebony locks.

"Nope."

"What kind of rake are you?" she teased playfully.

"I guess not a very good one." He snorted.

"We don't need condoms. I'm on the pill and I'm clean."

"Good, me too!"

Before she really understood what was happening, Koa had her naked on his bed and he was settling between her spread legs staring at her dripping wet sex.

"I'm gonna taste you," he growled.

The animalistic sound caused a sudden flood of liquid arousal to seep from her core.

"Right here."

Then he used the calloused tip of his middle finger to rub gentle circles over her throbbing clit.

"Then," he continued in a sexy Barry White sounding voice. "I'm gonna tongue-fuck this tight little pussy of yours until you scream my name."

He bent over and playfully nipped her inner thigh.

"And maybe if you're a good little Commander, I'll give you a *treat*."

Really? What kind of treat? Like a cookie… or maybe a—

But she didn't have much time to contemplate what he meant by a *'treat'* before Koa's head descended and began kissing, licking, and sucking the slippery nubbin at the apex of her sex.

"*Oh! My! Heavens!*" The steady suction of his mouth, teeth and tongue were quickly driving her to the brink of madness.

"Wait!" he said arrogantly. "There's more."

Before she could ask *what* he meant, the well-trained *sexpertise* gorging himself on her sex, stiffened his tongue like a spear and began thrusting the muscle in and out of her soaked folds. Over and over again. Stopping only momentarily to suck her labia completely into his hot mouth and licking her overly sensitive lower lips.

"*Mmm!*" she moaned, feeling the tingle in her belly but trying desperately to hold it off.

Koa must have felt it too because he commanded, "Don't come, not yet."

"I don't know if I can make that promise," she whispered with her eyes tightly shut.

"You will." He chuckled.

The man returned to his work stoking her passion, making her writhe against the cool cotton bed sheets beneath her. She felt the orgasm creeping up on her and stiffened, but Koa immediately pulled away drawing her away from her impending release.

"What are you doing?" Desperation filled her harshly spoken words.

"You'll see," he stated as he got on his knees, arranging her thighs over his broad, muscular shoulders and placing both of his hands on the globes of her ass, holding her up in midair. Without warning he dipped his head once again resuming his feast on her clit, making his way lower to her slick entrance to tongue-fuck her once again. Then after hearing an animalistic groan escape her, he made his way further down along the seam of her ass to her puckered hole.

"Has anyone ever fucked your ass?" he asked while rubbing the virgin entrance with his thumb.

"No," she answered breathlessly.

"Would you like to try?" She stiffened in panic. He kissed her thigh. "Don't worry I won't use my cock. Not now. Do you trust me?"

She nodded hesitantly.

"Good, just relax and enjoy your *treat*."

Koa bent his head again this time over her tight rosette. Slowly, he lapped the sensitive area, licking and tracing wide circles with his tongue, and as his circles became smaller and directly over her puckered entrance once again, he speared that talented muscle of his and began thrusting into her tight passage, hard and deep.

"*Oh my!*" she screamed with pleasure as he continued to take her… *there*… with hard wet jabs followed by the occasional lick, working her back entrance like he did her pussy.

It was the most deliciously wicked, sensuous thing she'd ever experienced, and it was amazing!

"I think I'm gonna come!" she announced loudly.

"Not yet." He shook his head again, resumed his position giving attention to her puckered hole, and then suddenly plunged three thick digits into her drenched sex.

The unexpected invasion sent her careening off the cliff.

The orgasm hit her like a semi-trailer. Hard and fast. Devastating her entire body, but before she could come back down to earth, Koa rested her back down on the mattress and plunged his cock inside her with one hard stroke.

"Damn it!" he yelled as she yelped, and he stopped immediately. "Did I hurt you?"

"Yes," she whispered. "You're too big. Maybe, you should take it out."

He took a slow cleansing breath before stating, "I'll take it slow. We'll make it fit. You're just so *tight* and hot. You feel incredible, kitten."

"I'm not that tight," she mumbled. "You're just enormous like an *anaconda*."

SEALING THE DEAL

He chuckled.

"You do wonders for my ego, kitten." He lowered to claim her already parted lips taking her with heartbreaking tenderness.

She hissed as he worked his thick, hard shaft further into her still spasming channel.

"I'm certain your ego was inflated enough without my comments."

Ignoring her playful insult, Koa began an unhurried advance and retreat into her sex, slowly parting her swollen muscles, in, out, in, out, in a steady rhythm that literally brought tears to her eyes.

"Watch me take you, Adrienne," he commanded as he pulled completely out of her.

Rising up on her elbows, she stared at where they were soon to be joined. Even in the darkened room she could see his cock was long, thick, and pulsing with veins. It was her fantasy come to life. Her mouth lost all moisture.

She gulped as his size truly registered in her brain.

"All of *that*, Lieutenant Commander," her eyes widened to the size of saucers as she gawked. "Should be against the laws of nature."

"Don't worry," he blushed. "I know how to use it."

Needing to touch him, Adrienne slid her trembling palms across Koa's massive chest, marveling at the feel of his smooth mocha skin stretched taut over muscles that were hard as granite. Those wise hazel eyes closed on a low groan, and his calloused hands pushed her hips further apart, his head falling back in a gesture of surrender that surprised and thrilled her. Koa was lost in her touches, relishing them, soaking them up like a sponge when she lingered in especially sensitive areas.

It was overwhelming, the sight of such a powerful and dangerous warrior turned to putty in her hands. And he was dangerous, of which she had no doubt. Still, there was something in his eyes and something in the way he moved, the aura of command in everything he did or said. This man, this regal Hawaiian prince was never truly at ease. Yet here he was, naked in every way and at her command.

It was intoxicating.

"Watch," he encouraged, his voice sounding strained as he took his long, thick cock in hand and tilted it down to enter her. It was the most erotic thing she'd ever seen.

His movements were so focused, so deliberate, and his wicked gaze riveted to where the smooth, mushroom-head of his cock was pressing into her. A muffled groan came out of her filled with three months' worth of pent-up longing and sexual tension. And as she watched, his magnificent cock was slowly pushing into her slick tissue, forcing it to give way to him.

She held her breath as she struggled to accept all of him. Whimpering as he slowly rolled his hips, sliding deeper into her tight, wet channel, filling not only her body, but her heart as well.

Reaching behind him, she grabbed his firm, tight bottom pulling him toward her while she pushed up. Unable to stop, she moaned at the pleasurable pain as he seated himself to the hilt, his weighty sack slapping against the seam of her butt.

"Ah!" he moaned. "There we go. How does it feel?"

"Amazing," she whispered, moving her hips in slow circular motions against his pelvis.

She was going out of her mind, and her body was ready to burst into flames. Eagerly, her sex clenched around the massive appendage throbbing inside her and she gritted her teeth from the pleasure of it.

"But I need you to move, Koa."

Finally, Koa began to move, withdrawing and advancing on every down stroke. Thrusting in slow, unhurried motions, driving her closer and closer to her orgasm. The man joined so intimately to her swiveled and plunged, in and out, over and over and over again. Under her palms, she felt Koa's ass clench and release as he continued to pump into her melting core, and she felt that delicious tingle in her sex building once again.

"Hurry, Koa!" She tried to squeeze her legs together to subdue the pleasure, but she was securely locked in place by his trunk-like legs. "I'm going to come!"

Koa came down on his elbows, eye-level with her rock-hard nipples.

"Offer these beauties up to me. Ah! Just like that," he smirked. "You look like a virgin offering herself up to some pagan deity, such perfect offerings."

He bent and graced one nipple with a slow wet glide of his tongue as she held her breasts up to his mouth.

"Mmm," he groaned. "So tasty. I'm gonna suck your nipples while I fuck your tight little pussy until you come. Does that sound good, kitten?"

"Yes!" she yelled, her back arching off of the mattress.

"So ripe, so ready for me. I could stay here like this... *all... night... long.*" He punctuated each word with a thrust of his hips. "But I'm gonna take you out of your misery."

She nodded, desperate to find release.

Taking mercy on her, the sex god began to stroke deeper. His balls slapped against the curve of her ass in a methodical rhythm, the sound only enhancing her pleasure. Koa's pace increased as he pistoned in and out of her with astonishing speed. Reaching between their bodies, he found that sensitive little bundle of nerves poking out of its hood and gently circled it with his fingers in time with his thrusts, pushing her into the sweetest ecstasy she'd ever experienced.

The second orgasm hit her even harder than the first. Causing her eyes to actually cross and she thought she might pass out from the sheer pleasure of it.

"One more time," he announced like he was commanding a battalion.

"*What?*" She gasped.

"One more time."

"No." She shook her head. "I can't. Not so soon."

"Yes," he ordered. "Don't think, just feel."

Before she could protest again, the insufferable man pumped through her spasms, slowing once again to that steady pace. Her mind reeled trying to understand how one person could have such stamina. It was totally beyond her comprehension.

After several moments, his pace increased again, grinding the root of his unrelenting cock against her pelvis. Adrienne felt his entire body stiffen and swell and grow to an impossible size. Then finally he plunged to the hilt, his cock nudging her cervix, he stilled as hot spurts of his seed emptied into her well-used sex, triggering a smaller orgasm that rolled through her in gentle waves.

"I've never felt anything so *good*," he gasped, his large body blanketing over hers with exhaustion.

His announcement made her grin.

"So… fucking… good," he repeated, continuing to claim her pussy with his semi-hard shaft.

Damn! The man was a sexual gladiator, the Zeus of orgasms.

Carefully, Koa rolled off of her, tucking her tired body against his still heaving chest.

"Kitten," he whispered.

"Hmm," was the only sound she could make as she glanced at the bedside clock, realizing they'd been at it for over an hour and a half.

Good God Almighty!

"How was it?"

"I think you wore-out my vagina." Adrienne giggled like a schoolgirl. "I'll have to purchase an extended warranty for it."

He laughed, making her pussy clench in that eager way.

"Tomorrow." He kissed her temple before closing his eyes. "I need sleep. I've got training in the morning."

And without another word, he fell fast asleep.

Exhausted from their escapade, she closed her eyes as well, wallowing in her euphoria before drifting into a well needed sleep.

CHAPTER SEVEN

Adrienne awoke to a disturbingly quiet house, but before she could panic, she noticed a note on the nightstand along with a glass of orange juice and a strawberry pop-tart. Immediately, she read the short note,

"Back around noon, had special training this morning. I'll bring back food. Don't get dressed."

She giggled to herself.

The bedside clock informed that it was almost ten-thirty in the morning. Koa will be back soon. Wanting to freshen up, she ran to the bathroom and quickly showered and brushed her teeth with an unopened toothbrush under the sink.

Her body was slightly sore. Why wouldn't it be since said body hadn't had sex in over a year and was now being used by a man who was hung like a stallion?

That rogue had given her multiple orgasms; *multiple freaking orgasms!* She never thought she could do that, never had the *chance* to do *that*. Adrienne smiled again as she towel-dried her body and grabbed one of Koa's Navy t-shirts from his dresser. Pulling it over her head, she noticed it smelled like him, lightly scented laundry detergent and cinnamon with a hint of citrus.

Lovely.

Actually, everything he owned was magnificent too. Glancing around the large master bedroom, Adrienne noticed his contemporary-styled space, furnished with a massive king-sized bed with leather-padded headboard, matching distressed oak dresser, two nightstands, and a hand-carved armoire housing a forty-two-inch flat screen television set.

Throughout the room hung framed original black and white photographs of different locations around the Hawaiian Islands including Koko Crater, Mt. Kilauea, and the North Shore. She wondered if Koa had taken the photos. If so, the man was a talented photographer.

Needing to fix her hair, Adrienne found a wide-toothed comb on his dresser and combed out her tangles while sipping her orange juice and gobbling down her strawberry-flavored *Pop-Tart*. Who knew amazing sex could make you so hungry.

Outside, the muffled sounds of gently lapping waves against the shore, combined with the happy shrills of overhead gulls serenaded her, beckoning her to go out onto the balcony.

Releasing the lock, she pulled open the sliding glass door and stepped out onto the small space. The view of the *Moks* from Koa's balcony was incredible. Inhaling deeply, she reveled in the crisp salt-scented breeze coming off the choppy Pacific.

"Mmm," she sighed.

A girl could get used to waking up like this every morning, sated, content and cherished.

"I see you've been a bad girl." The deep, raspy baritone startled her back to reality.

Turning quickly, she locked gazes with a very disgruntled Navy SEAL looking sexier than ever. Damp black hair slicked back away from his attractive face, eyes-tinged red from a late night and an early morning, wearing dark, knee-length shorts and a white tank top with the U.S. Navy logo on it.

"I guess I'll have to punish you," he chuckled, waggling his brows.

Koa had broken every speeding law ever written in his haste to get back to the gloriously naked sleeping goddess he had left in the wee hours of the morning. All day, his overactive imagination bombarded him with lustful thoughts of her begging and squealing as he pumped his cock inside of her slick pussy. The naughty images had made him semi-erect all morning long.

Adrienne's brow arched.

"How am I a bad girl?" she feigned innocence, batting her thick dark lashes.

He swallowed hard, before answering.

"I told you not to get dressed."

"Huh?" She tapped her bottom lip as if deep in thought. "I must have forgotten."

Then she pouted, her sexy expression hardening his impatient cock even more.

"Bring that sexy body over here, temptress." Koa held out his hand.

To his surprise, Adrienne did as she was told and sauntered toward him, swaying her t-shirt covered hips seductively. His shirt looked like a dress on her petite form reaching her just above the knees, but she still looked like pure sin.

His cock hardened more, its stiff form tenting his swim trunks.

"What kind of punishment do you have in mind?" She grinned.

He chuckled maniacally like an evil villain and pulled her toward one of the Adirondack chairs on the balcony, sitting down first before pulling her onto his lap to straddle him—hazel eyes to green.

"Are you sore?" he asked, knowing he had ridden her hard the night before. Around her, he just couldn't control himself. It was as if she brought out every caveman compulsion buried deep within him.

"Just a little." She mischievously pouted.

Gently, he smoothed his hand down her back and slid his fingers over the top of her bottom.

"I don't want to hurt you, but I just can't seem to get enough," the man confessed sincerely, his words tugging at her soul.

Adrienne's breath hitched, as he angled his head to kiss her, lightly brushing against her mouth with feather-soft pressure.

"We don't have to do anything you don't want to," he reassured, caressing her cheek with his thumb. "We can spend the day on the beach. I'll grill some steaks later."

She cupped his face with both hands, using her thumbs to smooth his eyebrows. The action soothed him for some unknown reason, making him press into her gentle touch. He maneuvered his hand beneath her t-shirt instantly locating her neatly trimmed curls, his semi-hard member immediately jumped to attention as he slid one finger between her pussy folds and felt the evidence of her arousal.

"You're always so wet for me," he moaned.

"I can't help it," was her only reply.

At his request, *his* woman leaned back, her body relaxing on his lap, giving him the opportunity to push his finger even deeper, as her inner muscles gripped him like a vise.

At his ministrations, Adrienne suddenly stiffened.

"Suppose someone sees us?" she gasped in horror.

"They won't," Koa reassured. "The wooden slats that make up the deck walls are only one inch apart. I promise no one will be able to see what we're doing."

Then he slowly raised her shirt with one hand and palmed one breast using his thumb to gently flick the already stiff nipple. Instantly she soaked his still embedded finger with cream.

"You are so naughty," he purred. "I'm soaked with your cream."

"I'm not the naughty one," she moaned on a gasp.

Quite unexpectedly, the highly trained frogman caught movement on the beach below and stilled his movements.

"What's wrong?" Adrienne spoke in a hushed tone.

He smiled wickedly, removing his slippery finger from her core.

"I think we're being watched," he said.

Terrified at the thought of someone seeing her in this condition, she tried to pull her shirt back over her naked breasts, but he wouldn't let her.

"Don't worry," Koa soothed. "I told you they can't see anything."

Then he pulled her against his body, sealing his lips over hers and smashing their chests together. Releasing her shirt, he slid his hands down her back to fondle her firm, round ass. Instinctively he pushed upward, finding his way blocked by his still damp swimming trunks.

"Pull out my cock, kitten."

Longing to be inside her, he leaned forward to kiss a line from her collarbone to her left earlobe. He grinned when she reached between them, drove her hand inside the waistband of his trunks and freed his painfully erect member.

Just as needy, Adrienne held him firmly at the base of his shaft and pumped him from root to tip… once, twice, thrice.

"That feels so good, kitten. Maybe you should give it a little kiss." His voice sounded weak and raspy and sinfully seductive.

To his surprise, she scooted further back on his lap and leaned forward giving the smooth tip of his cock a slow, wet glide with her tongue, circling the head like a lollipop.

"Mmm," she groaned against the engorged head. "Yummy."

Before he could urge her to do it again, she took half of his thick, long rod into her mouth using her tongue to caress the sensitive underside below the head.

"Fuck!"

He bucked upward propelling him further inside her warm, wet cavern, sucking him like he was her favorite treat. Expertly, she continued to pump his shaft as her mouth, teeth, and tongue worked their magic pulling him closer to his impending orgasm.

"Stop, Adrienne," he begged his seductress. "I don't want to come in your mouth, not now. Put my cock inside of you."

Obediently, she followed his instructions, lifting and positioning him at the entrance to her soaked sex. Gradually, lowering her body onto his, taking him in, one hard inch at a time until she'd buried his cock deep.

"Mmm, you feel amazing," she softly mewled into his ear.

"You're gonna kill me, kitten," he grinned. "But what a way to go."

More in control in this position, Adrienne placed her hands on his shoulders and began riding him with slow, smooth strokes. Instinctively, he leaned forward again and sucked one of her nipples into his mouth along with the cotton material covering the large, firm mounds. Another gasp escaped her lips at the additional stimulation.

"I can't hold it for much longer," she whimpered.

"Fuck me, then," he commanded. "Make me explode with you."

His whole body began to shake when the woman of his dreams moaned and increased her pace. All he could do was brace his feet on the wooden floor and push upward over a dozen times, fucking her tight pussy with powerful thrusts. Enjoying how her large breasts jiggled with every motion urging him on like silent cheerleaders.

"Koa," she moaned.

Suddenly, her entire body stiffened, and he felt her inner muscles pulsing around his pistoning cock, forcing his seed to the top of his sensitive tip.

"That's it, kitten," he encouraged, "I'm right… there… with you!"

And he was. Suddenly, the base of his spine began to tingle, his balls drew up into tight fists, and then a hard burst of hot liquid jetted out of his member with a force that took his breath away.

"Adrienne!" Her name rushed past his lips like a mantra as he repeated it over and over again until his breathing went back to normal, and he began to soften inside of her. Exhausted from their morning workout, he chuckled.

"What's so funny?" Adrienne demanded; their bodies still pressed firmly together.

"I think you broke my penis," he groaned, pulling his re-hardening appendage out of her juicy womanhood.

Laughter burst from her lungs.

"Don't laugh," he chastised playfully. "If it's broken, how will I, you know."

"Hmm," she pouted. "Then I guess I'd better fix it."

She leaned down once again and took his cock into her mouth.

"Mmm," he groaned. *"Such a naughty, naughty girl."*

"This is delectable." Adrienne took a healthy bite without shame.

The lingering deliciousness of the crispy fried spring roll, making her moan with delight.

"Who made this?" she licked her lips, not caring how it looked.

"My mom," Koa informed with pride, popping a fried shrimp into his mouth.

"Really?"

"Yeah, my parents own several food trucks, and one so happened to be at the beach the team trains at."

"Can *you* cook?" she asked, taking a shrimp off his plate without asking.

"Of course, I can," the man smirked. "My parents taught me and my sister when we were kids. Our parttime jobs were helping on the food trucks."

"I'll believe it when I see it," she chuckled, riling him up.

"Challenge taken; I'll whip you up something mouthwatering for dinner tonight."

"Is that so," she grinned. "It's very presumptuous of you to think I'm going to stay another night and let you have your wicked way with me."

Koa pouted and it was the sexiest thing she'd seen in forever.

"Fine, then leave me here all alone with my lascivious thoughts," he impishly countered. "Who knows what sort of trouble I'll get into?"

She rolled her eyes trying desperately to keep a neutral face.

"Uh huh! I can only imagine," she ribbed then giggled, unable to hold it inside any longer.

The man was such a menace.

"May I ask you a question?" her handsome companion queried.

Koa sat up on the red and white checkered picnic blanket they were lounging on, enjoying their snack and the azure beauty of the ocean. It was almost sunset, and the lowering sun painted the sky with shades of persimmon, gold and amethyst. It took her breath away.

"Go ahead." She popped another grape into her mouth, moaning at the tangy sweetness.

"Why haven't you told me anything about your past?"

"I have," she said in her defense.

He shook his head.

"No, you've told me about all of the different places you've been stationed. That's not the same thing."

Adrienne hesitated for several long, tense moments before responding.

"Well," she glanced around nervously, clearing her throat several times, and began packing up their uneaten items. "I was raised for a few years in a French city called *Calais*. Have you heard of it?"

"Sure," he smiled. "I actually took the hovercraft over from Dover, England to Calais. I even stayed the night. They have awesome food too."

"You are always thinking with your stomach," she chuckled; he was always contemplating on his next meal.

"So, you're French?" Koa grinned.

"No, I'm American," she clarified. "I was born at a base in Naples, Italy, but I grew up all over really, a Navy brat I guess you'd call me. I've lived in several European countries. I was in Singapore for a while. Also, Maryland, California, American Samoa, and now, here."

"What are your parents like?" he questioned, wanting to know everything about her.

She sat straighter trying to maintain her composure.

"My father's family is from American Samoa," she patiently educated. "That's why I wanted to be stationed there. I needed to see where he grew up. I have a few family members who still live there. I've gotten closer to them during the two years I was there."

"Oh," he acknowledged, listening intently.

"My father was Samoan, a descendant of the island's royal family actually. He was a very large man, tall and broad-shouldered, with the kindest chocolate brown eyes. I have his skin coloring. You kind of remind me of him," she added with a smirk. "My mother was French, born and raised in Calais. She was a petite woman, only five-two, but she was a spitfire, who had long chestnut-brown hair and bright green eyes. Just like me. They met while my father was stationed in Europe. They fell in love and married within six months, one of those fairytale love stories."

"You're describing them in the past tense as if—" Koa's brow arched, and his eyes narrowed.

She couldn't help the tear that escaped, rolling mockingly down her cheek.

Damn it!

She didn't want to cry in front of him like some sort of over-emotional female. Which was exactly what she looked like at the moment.

"They drowned when I was ten." She began to feel more of those traitorous tears in their watery descent. "Went out on a fishing trip and never came back. My maternal grandparents raised me after that and when I turned eighteen, I went to college, got my degree in engineering then enlisted in the Navy, like my father."

Wanting to comfort her, he grabbed her hand and tugged her into his lap, tucking her head into the crook of his neck. Relaxing a little, she inhaled deeply, then drew in the scent of cinnamon, citrus, and Koa's unique fragrance.

"Adrienne, I'm so sorry," he whispered, cradling her against his broad, muscled chest. "Do you have any brothers or sisters?"

On the brink of tears, she shook her head no.

"It took my mom three years to finally get pregnant with me," the woman sniffled. "I'm not sure if they ever tried to have any more children after I was born."

"Do you still keep in touch with your grandparents?" he asked, changing the subject.

"My grandfather passed away a couple of years ago, but my grandmother still lives in Calais. I talk to her every Sunday and visit when I can."

"I can't imagine what you went through," Koa sighed with a heavy heart. "If my parents… well, I don't even want to imagine anything like that happening."

"I wouldn't either," she stated confidently. "Your mom and dad, your entire family is wonderful."

"Yeah, I think so too," he agreed with a chuckle and then he stood and lifted them both to their feet. "C'mon up to the house and I'll make you some dinner."

"Trying to woo me with food, are you?" she snickered.

He blushed before he replied.

"That was the plan."

The fully restored three-bedroom two bath 1930's beachside bungalow was immaculate to say the least. After all, he prided himself on being neat and organized. The military had drilled that into him from the first day of basic training.

He decorated the space himself, with only a few minor suggestions from his mom and sister. His cousin Noelani helped him choose the color scheme and assisted in furniture placement. Since he was a guy, he didn't care about how things coordinated or clashed in a space, let alone how to achieve a consistent flow from room to room.

Thank goodness the women in his family did.

In the living room, his furnishings were minimal consisting of a full-sized cream leather sectional sofa, paired with a hand-made driftwood coffee table he had constructed himself. Miraculously, he had found the battered piece of wood on the shore outside of his house a couple of years back. Everything he couldn't make himself, he purchased on *eBay* or specialty online vendors, but his one true indulgence was a gigantic sixty-inch, flat-screen television, which he saved for nearly a year. It was his only *'guy'* purchase.

A custom-made shelving unit, he and his father built, ran along the entire back wall of the living room, housing an array of books ranging from the official biography of *Martin Luther King, Jr.* to *James Patterson's* latest thriller. Vintage laser disks including old-school *To Kill a Mockingbird* starring Gregory Peck to nature documentaries, a huge collection of *Blu-ray*s, and antique Hawaiian artifacts, pottery, and tribal masks he had collected from family members and auctions. The entire wrap-around unit flanked three floor-to-ceiling picture windows overlooking the Pacific Ocean outback.

Several months ago, he had installed new double French doors that led out to the screened in lanai. After a tough day of training or an unsavory mission, he would lounge in the space while warm tropical trade winds washed over him. Many nights he would let the sound of the surf ferry him off to dreamland and wake the next morning to a 180-degree-view of a fiery sunrise of crimson, bronze, and cerulean.

This was Hawai'i at its best and he wouldn't trade it for the world.

"I love these floors." Adrienne glanced around the room in admiration.

"Me too. They're the original Douglas fir flooring," Koa stated proudly. "It had to be shipped over from the mainland then painstakingly stripped, sanded, and refinished which took a hell of a lot of man-hours, late nights, and weekends, but the end result couldn't be debated. It was well worth the calluses and splinters."

He informed even the kitchen got an overhaul with new sealed concrete countertops, polished mahogany cabinets, dual farmhouse sinks and all new stainless-steel appliances. He had even expanded the small pantry into a walk-in one allowing him to buy in bulk. There was also enough room to build a small alcove for a washer and dryer.

All the interior walls of the bungalow were painted white and depended upon the pops of color from the furniture and accessories to add interest and personality. The house was the perfect representation of him, and he loved everything about it.

She let out a low whistle.

"Color me impressed," she mumbled under her breath. "It is stunning. I didn't really get a chance to look around the other night… you know… with all of the—"

"Fucking," he chuckled devilishly as he continued to chop the onions, celery, and garlic.

Adrienne made a funny face, making him burst out laughing.

"Must you be so crass?" she blushed.

"Yes, I must. It's ingrained in my DNA."

"You're ridiculous." She giggled and it was the sweetest thing he had heard in a long time.

"Do you want the grand tour after dinner?" he volunteered.

"Thanks, I'd love to see the rest of the place."

"What are we doing tonight? Watching TV?" Koa noticed her eyes glancing across at the movie theatre sized flat screen. "It's impressive, right?"

"Are you trying to compensate for something?" She teased as she blatantly glanced down at his quickly growing member, licking her lips as it tented his shorts.

He laughed enjoying their flirtatious banter.

"I don't know. Am I?" One eyebrow winged up. She only blushed, ignoring his comment.

"I think dinner and a movie is the way to go," she agreed, trying not to look at his pants again.

Koa smiled to himself; the woman was just too damn adorable.

SEALING THE DEAL

"Go ahead you can say it," Koa chuckled, loudly. "I already know."

Adrienne rolled her mesmerizing green eyes, licking the last of the powdered sugar off of her fingertips. "Okay, you win. Dinner was better than sex."

"I wouldn't go that far, but yeah, I thought it was tasty." His brow arched.

"More than tasty," she practically purred her appreciation.

Koa had gone all out trying to impress her, whipping up lobster, crab, and corn chowder garnished with crispy pancetta, freshly baked rosemary-parmesan focaccia, and pineapple upside-down cake dusted with powdered sugar for dessert.

Even he was impressed.

"Wow! I'll never doubt your culinary prowess again, Lieutenant Commander Kapahu," she complimented, grinning profusely.

"Make sure you don't, Commander Mathis," he teased, while loading up the dishwasher as Adrienne wiped off the breakfast bar.

Their comfortable way with each other soothing his anxiety, he wanted her so badly that his groin was on high alert, but after hearing her tragic history he didn't want her to think he was taking advantage of her delicate state. When she accidentally rubbed against his groin as she added another dirty dish to the machine, he thought he'd explode in his pants.

"Holy cow!" She glanced at his bulge, blushing at the feel of his hard cock against her bottom.

All he could do was grin.

"You, Sir," she giggled. "Are insatiable. Doesn't your *'anaconda'* ever get tired?"

"Apparently not when you're around." He turned deep red.

Adrienne sighed; the sound filled with contentment.

"What about work tomorrow?"

"I'll set the alarm, so you have enough time to go home for some clean clothes," her host relayed.

"Okay." She held his hand like a little child, her green eyes almost glowing in the dim space.

Sweetly, he took her hand at the same time turning off the light and led her down the hall to his bedroom. Quickly, he undressed her and replaced her clothes with one of his clean t-shirts before changing into a pair of loose-fitting striped pajama bottoms that hung low around his hips.

"Koa," she said with a breathless whisper.

"Yeah, kitten?"

"I want you." She swallowed, hard, the sound making his cock flex in his pants.

"No sex tonight," Koa informed as they climbed into bed. Pulling her against him, her back to his chest, his hard length pressed against her ass, but she didn't protest only snuggled against him and fell asleep, leaving him to ponder what the hell he was doing.

She was so small compared to him, but they fit together like two halves of a whole.

Koa *loved* the scent of lilac that surrounded her. He *loved* the way she made faces at his corny jokes but still laughed. He *loved* how she babbled when she got nervous, which was often. He *loved* how they could sit together in comfortable silence without feeling uncomfortable. He especially *loved* the way she said his name with a hint of a French accent. It always warmed his soul.

And the sex.

Damn!

The woman could milk him like a dairy cow and five minutes later she'd be ready to milk him again. Adrienne was his other half and he adored her. Without a doubt. He knew it with every fiber of his being, and the realization didn't terrify him. It made him smile.

He just hoped she felt the same.

CHAPTER EIGHT

"You promised," Koa stated firmly.

"It was made under duress."

He laughed arrogantly; a smug smile plastered all over his delectable face. "My ass!"

Adrienne rolled her eyes; the man was insufferable.

"Why do I have to say it?"

"Because saying it will make me feel good," he smirked in that boyish way of his, making her heart melt like a popsicle in July.

"But you already know," she huffed loudly.

"Just say it," he pressed without heat.

Rolling her eyes again, she said in a bored, flat, emotionless tone.

"Lieutenant Commander Koa, you are amazing! The Polynesian god of sexual delight! The *Shaolin* master of everything *below* the neck. I adore you and your—" she stopped in mid-sentence.

"Say it," he chuckled. "That was the bet. You said if I could give you *four* orgasms in a row in less than thirty minutes, you promised to say it."

He narrowed his eyes playfully, daring her not to.

"C'mon, kitten," he urged. "Say it."

Adrienne cleared her throat.

"I adore you and your *twelve-inch* anaconda."

"See." He leaned back against the padded headboard, eyes closed, with her straddling his hips, her cheek over his heart, listening to the strong, rhythmic beat. "That wasn't so bad."

"Maybe for you," she complained with mock shame. "But for me it was worse than eating liver."

"*Yuck!*" he grimaced.

"Exactly," she smiled to herself, loving his carefree nature.

It had been a week since they last made love, and she couldn't imagine it being any better. The man had the stamina of a stallion. It didn't hurt that he was hung like one too. They had spent almost the entire Saturday in bed only leaving to use the bathroom, shower, or eat.

"Are you ready for round *five*?" Koa opened one hazel eye to assess her mood. "You can be on top this time."

"I can't," she said, rolling off of him.

"Why?"

"Because I've got an appointment in an hour," she replied, while retrieving her panties from on top of the ceiling fan, unsure of how they even got there.

"Who with?" He sat up straighter, the movement causing the sheet to fall lower almost exposing his semi-hard member to her greedy gaze.

Focus Adrienne, focus!

Staying on task, she grabbed a clean towel from his laundry basket and started walking towards the ensuite bathroom.

"If you must know, I'm meeting with a realtor."

One brow arched in confusion.

"Why do you need a realtor? Is something wrong with your apartment?"

She shook her head.

"Nothing is wrong, per se," she explained. "I'm just ready to find something more permanent."

"I understand completely," he replied with a neutral tone. "Something permanent would be great."

He was staring at her strangely, eyes glistening with emotion.

"Why are you looking at me like that?"

"You don't need a realtor," the tough yet thoughtful Sailor stated matter-of-factly.

"And why is that?" she questioned as she tried to locate her bra.

Suddenly, he jumped out of bed and walked to his dresser, pulling something small out of his underwear drawer. All of his exquisite nakedness revealed to her salivating tongue.

Saints alive!

It should be illegal for one person to look that good. Her hand went to her mouth instinctively to check for any drool.

"Because I want you to live here with me," he clarified, his broad smile blinding her, sending little spasms from her heart to her nipples down to her dampening sex.

"I don't want to be your live-in sex-bot." she mumbled, shaking her head.

Ignoring her comment, Koa walked over to where she stood, naked, towel firmly grasped in her trembling hands, while he was also still gloriously naked. When he reached her, he got down on one knee, and presented her with a small, black velvet-covered box.

"What's this?" she gulped, trying to control her now shaking legs.

He grinned, that boyish one she loved.

"I bought it last week," he confessed gazing up at her. "It's been burning a hole in my pocket ever since. I've been trying to figure out some grand gesture to show how much I love you—"

"You *love* me?" She felt her heart almost lunge out of her chest. "Koa?"

"I do, kitten, with my entire heart. But you've forced my hand and I guess I'll just have to wing it."

"What's happening?" she closed her eyes, hoping to wake from this dream.

"Adrienne Louise Mathis," he began, looking up at her, his face filled with unspoken emotions. "I can't picture spending the next fifty years with anyone else but you. Every day we spend together I'm more certain that we belong together. *I love you.* Will you marry me?"

Then he slowly opened the box to reveal a flawless one and a half carat emerald flanked by two perfect trillion-cut diamonds all nestled in a platinum setting. It was the ring she would have picked out if she ever had to pick an engagement ring for herself.

"It's beautiful!" she gasped, trying to hold back the tears.

"So?" He tickled her knees bringing her back to reality. "Will you marry me?"

She swallowed, hard, cleared her throat several times, before saying, "Koa, I can't."

His face immediately fell.

"Why?" he asked, rising to a standing position.

Koa the rake had disappeared and was replaced by Lieutenant Commander Koa Joseph Kapahu, Navy SEAL.

Suddenly, she was faced with every intimidating inch of him. The highly trained Sailor, with his naked 6'7" chiseled form, broad shoulders blocking out everything behind him with a confused expression that stole her breath and made her forget how to breathe. She wasn't afraid of him. He'd never hurt her. Of that she was certain of, but his show of power instinctively made her military persona decide to make an appearance, and she wasn't one to back down either.

Adrienne stood straighter forgetting she was still naked and was about to go toe-to-toe with a very pissed-off warrior.

"We've only known each other for a few months," she stated emotionless. "I don't believe we know each other well enough to get married."

"Your parents did it, you said so yourself."

"We are not my parents," she growled.

"My parents did it and they've been married for nearly thirty-three years, and they still chase each other around the house when they think no one else is at home."

"We are not your parents either, Koa."

"I never claimed we were," his words rushed past dry lips. "I just mean that I want that with you. I want to chase you around the kitchen and wrestle with you under the covers. I want to raise little green-eyed, peanut-butter-colored future Navy SEALS with you. I want to have the same thing my parents have, and I want it with you."

"I'm not ready to settle down, Koa," her voice stayed steady.

"Is it the whole cheating thing that you went through with your last boyfriend? Is that why you don't want me? Because I'm *not* that asshole." He rubbed his head in a frustrated gesture. "I would never, could never, cheat on you."

"I realized that a while ago," she agreed. "You are wonderful, kind, and considerate. Why can't we wait for a few more years, until we're really ready?"

"What happens a year from now if you decide you're still not ready to get married, what then?"

"I don't know," she huffed with frustration.

"I don't want to waste any more time dating when I've found the woman I love and want to start a family soon."

"So, you want me as a baby maker?!"

"That's not what I meant, and you know it."

He walked over to the bed, grabbed his discarded shorts and t-shirt quickly donning them before pulling on a pair of socks and slipping on his sneakers.

"Do you love me?" he continued, staring down at her.

"What—"

"Do. You. Love. Me?"

"I… I don't know," she whispered.

He frowned, suddenly uncomfortable.

"Then it all makes sense," he said, sarcasm lacing his words.

"Can we still see each other as friends?" The question rushed out before she could stop them.

He laughed, the sound resembling fingernails drawn down a chalkboard.

"I'm not a doormat or a glutton for punishment and I think way too much of myself to chase after someone who doesn't want to be caught."

"Where are you going?" She looked at him curiously.

"I'm going for a run on the beach," the ticked-off man stated without looking at her.

"You're going for a run, right now?"

"Lock the door behind you when you leave. I'll grab my keys on my way out."

With that said, he left the room without another word, leaving her standing in the middle of his bedroom wondering what happened to her amazing weekend.

CHAPTER NINE

Ring! Ring! Ring!

"*Aloha.*"

"Hello, Kai." Adrienne's voice was barely a whisper.

"Hi, Adrienne, how are you?"

"Not well," she sniffled. "Is your brother there?"

Koa shook his head vehemently.

"No," Kai lied. "Have you tried calling his cell?"

"He's not answering."

"I'm sorry." Kai glanced over at her brother who was sitting on her sofa looking like a lost puppy. "Do you want me to give him a message when I see him?"

"Kai," Adrienne chuckled, her voice sounding muffled on the other end. "You are a lot of things, but a good liar you are not."

"Sorry," she sighed. "What should I tell him?"

There was a long, pregnant pause before she answered.

"Tell him... I miss him and wondered if he'd like to meet, to talk?"

"Koa?"

Her brother shook his head no, before exiting the room

"I'm sorry, Adrienne, but he's not ready to see you quite yet."

"Okay, thank you," she whimpered before hanging up.

Kai went to find her brother who had suddenly vanished.

"Where's Uncle Koa?" she asked her little boy who was eating a grilled ham and cheese sandwich.

"He left," A.J. replied, before taking another bite out of the half-eaten snack. "He told me to tell you goodbye."

Koa's house just seemed quieter than usual, lonely and it was making him crazy.

It had been a long week of avoiding Adrienne around the base, dodging her phone calls at home and at the office, and trying not to go insane with the need to beg her to give him any scraps of her affection she deemed enough. She'd even tracked him down at his deep-sea rescue training class earlier in the week, but he completely ignored her, so she finally gave up.

The inclement weather for the past few days didn't help to ease his anxiety. A typhoon was heading toward the islands and all travel to and from the mainland had been canceled. At the base, emergency protocols were activated, and he was on-call until the storm passed.

As he sat contemplating his lack of a love life, there was a gentle knock on the door, and without thought, he jogged over to the front door and pulled it open. Surprised to see the gorgeous Commander on his doorstep. Her green eyes red and puffy, button nose slightly pink, and looking as miserable as he felt.

"Please, Koa," her voice raspy as if she'd been crying non-stop all week. "Don't send me away."

His heart thumping with excitement, but he told it to shut up.

"I just want to talk." She sniffled.

He looked her over, trying to suppress the urge to grab her around the waist, pull her against his chest, and kiss her until she couldn't remember her own name. Instead, he opened the door further and allowed her to enter before closing the door behind her.

"Sit down," he insisted, pointing to the leather sectional.

Without complaint, she did as she was told.

"Would you like something to drink or maybe something to eat?"

Adrienne looked as if she hadn't eaten in a while and the realization concerned him.

"I'm not hungry or thirsty, but thanks."

She smiled before sweeping over the room, her gaze lingering on the Pacific outside.

"I miss the peacefulness here, with you," she confessed.

Koa's brow arched, his heartbeat speeding up fueled with hope.

"Why are you here, Commander?"

"I've missed you," she confessed with weepy eyes.

He couldn't help the smile that spread across his face.

"I've missed you too."

Then he stood suddenly crossing the short distance between them and tugged her gently into his arms. She felt so good. Hugging her lush curves, he buried his nose in her loose chestnut strands, inhaling deeply the faint scent of lilac and her unique aroma.

"You're killing me, Adrienne. I can't sleep or eat or function. The men in my unit are threatening to throw me overboard on the next deep-sea mission."

She rested her cheek against his chest as they stood holding each other.

"I feel the same way," she revealed with pout. "Aiden has even given me a few dirty looks this week."

"Adrienne," Koa whispered against her hair. *"Is this a yes?"*

He felt her small body stiffen and he knew what she wouldn't say.

"I see," he said flatly. "This must be a bootie call."

Before she could answer his cell phone rang.

"Aloha," he greeted politely, still looking at her. "When did this happen? Okay, I'll be there in less than an hour. Make sure they're in full gear, *Mahalo.*"

He put his phone in his pocket then grabbed the keys to his SUV.

"I have to go."

"Where are you going?" Adrienne demanded, wanting to clear the air. "It's storming outside. Plus, it's a weekend."

"It's classified," he simply stated. "If you want to wait out the storm here, feel free, but you can't just keep showing up. You know what I want from you, Adrienne, and if you don't feel the same way about me, then it's not fair to lead me on. I love you, but please… just leave me alone."

He left the house, instinctively making sure his dog tags were around his neck then, as was his custom, quickly called his parents and sister to say goodbye just in case he didn't return. It was no secret that sometimes when he was called to active status, that there was always a chance he might not make it back in one piece or at all.

He didn't like to dwell on it, but it was something that came with the job.

Adrienne's cell phone rang, bringing her back to the present.

"Hello, this is Commander Mathis."

"*Aloha*, Commander Mathis, this is Lieutenant Choy. Sorry to disturb you Ma'am." The unseen Sailor sounded emotionless on the other end. "But there's been a situation off the coast of Kauai. You'll need to report to base for debriefing ASAP."

"I'll be there in an hour, Lieutenant," she replied, her mind back in military mode. "Has Admiral Jameson been alerted?"

"Yes Ma'am."

"Good, I'm on my way."

CHAPTER TEN

Thank goodness the traffic on Kamehameha Highway was nonexistent. Adrienne navigated the roads carefully, but faster than she would normally in this type of weather. The rain was coming down in buckets, making the road slippery and dangerous.

Relief filled her as she checked in with the guard on duty at the entrance of the Navy base. The man verified her ID then quickly waved her through. Wasting no time, she parked in the officers' parking lot and by the time she made it to the command center she was drenched.

At almost twenty-three hundred hours she followed Admiral Jameson's assistant, Lieutenant Richards— for the life of her, she couldn't remember the young officer's first name and at the moment it wasn't relevant— through the vacant lobby of a two-story office building located at the edge of the base near the shipyard.

"Everyone is in the C and C, Commander. This way please," he spoke pleasantly even though his gray eyes were tinged red, probably due to lack of sleep or worry. "You'll need your ID badge to enter the more secured rooms, Ma'am."

"Sure," she said, pulling her badge out of her purse.

Rapidly, they walked down a long, narrow, well-lit hallway with glass walls and empty, dark conference rooms on either side. Then turned the corner and encountered two heavily armed guards standing on either side of an elevator.

"Badges, please." The taller, darker complexioned guard examined their identification cards and then motioned for them to swipe the cards into the reader. A green light appeared on the keypad, and they stepped inside the now opened elevator.

The Lieutenant pressed the down button, and she realized that the main command center must be hidden underground. After a short ride down, the doors slid open. As they stepped out, she felt a tightening in her chest and rubbed it discreetly. Something was horribly wrong, and she was about to be thrown in the middle of it.

They continued through the eerily quiet halls in silence. The twisting hallways reminded her of an ancient Grecian labyrinth. Visions of a vicious Minotaur and sadistic satyrs bombarded her overly active imagination, and she couldn't suppress the low giggle that seeped from her throat.

"Sorry." She grinned at the Lieutenant.

Cordially, the man smiled back, easing her tension.

"It's okay, Ma'am. The tension always makes me nervous as well."

Finally, they reached a thick metal door with a similar keypad located next to it.

"Ma'am, go ahead and swipe your badge then punch in the PIN number you selected during orientation.

It took her a few seconds to recall the code before punching several numbers into the keypad. The device beeped, turned green, and the panel door slid open revealing the heart of the command center. The sheer size of it took her breath away.

"Ready, Ma'am?" Lieutenant Richards asked.

"As I'll ever be," she replied.

Getting her bearings, Adrienne paused in the doorway and looked down at her wet clothing. Realization hit that she was wearing jeans and a T-shirt and mentally prayed that she wasn't the only one at the meeting dressed in civilian attire.

"Ma'am, I could wrangle you up something dry to wear," Richards Texas drawl came to the surface.

"Thank you, I'd appreciate it," she smiled.

She blew out a breath of relief when she entered the command center and saw everyone in attendance, including the senior Admiral sporting faded blue jeans and an *I Heart Hawai'i* T-shirt. The others wore everything from sweats to shorts and T-shirts.

Thank goodness!

"Commander Mathis." The silver-haired Admiral shook her hand then motioned for her to sit down at the conference table along with three other high-ranking officers and a civilian she'd never met.

"Sorry to have to bring you out of doors during this kind of weather," the Admiral began. "But I'm afraid we have a bit of a situation that needs to be dealt with quickly and discreetly."

As he was about to explain, another aide approached, whispered something in his ear, and waited for a response. After a moment he motioned for the group to follow him into an adjoining area.

SEALING THE DEAL

While they waited, Admiral Jameson's assistant waved them into a large, stadium-style room. Inside, there were four levels, each one about ten feet wide. Each level had a station every few feet housing a computer system and monitors, and a person calmly speaking on a headset or entering data via keyboard. A massive floor-to-ceiling monitor was situated in the front of the room displaying an infrared satellite feed with small, moving, colored dots and a ticker-tape-like message running along the bottom of the screen.

Quickly, Admiral Jameson introduced himself and then her to the group. She then sat and introduced herself to the others, and then anxiously waited while the Admiral began his briefing.

"At approximately twenty hundred hours today, the Coast Guard cruiser patrolling the coast of Kauai contacted their headquarters reporting two unmarked-unknown vessels transferring materials. During the call, the communications officer heard gunfire in the background then all communications ceased, and the ship's GPS locator was disarmed. Admiral Baker contacted me a little over an hour ago to request assistance. All he knew was whoever commandeered their ship is armed and has the means and knowledge to manipulate our technology."

"Can we track them by satellite?" Commander Marcia Elliot, Naval liaison of the Pacific Rim bases asked, her dark brown eyes narrowed intently.

"My IT people are working on it, but it seems they are using a secondary jamming device." Commander Gopaul's, head of the Information Technology department on base, soothing tone lulled the group into a more confident state.

Lieutenant Choy has been monitoring all communications channels for anything out of the ordinary and we've deployed a submarine to their last known location on recon. The SEAL team will be delivered to the Kauai location via sub,"

"Who did we deploy, Sir?" Adrienne asked, feeling a sudden gnawing in the pit of her stomach.

"Seal Delivery Vehicle Team ONE," their leader informed with great confidence. "Commander Kapahu's unit. They're the best unit in the Pacific, hands-down. They've been on more missions than I can count, and they've got a zero-casualty record for the last six years."

She heard the air rush out of her lungs like they were deflating, and it took all of her strength not to faint.

"The entire unit was deployed?" she managed to say. "When Sir?"

The older man glanced at the clock on the far wall.

"Fifteen minutes ago, give or take a few minutes," he surmised with a nod. "It will take them a little over an hour to reach the Coast Guard ship's last known coordinates in this weather, but they should be contacting command central as soon as they reach their destination."

"Oh," was the only thing she could say.

Suddenly, she remembered the call Koa had received during their talk.

Clearing her throat, she inquired, "What's my position on this, Sir?"

Admiral Jameson gave her a reassuring smile.

"I know your job on base is overseeing all engineering departments, Commander Mathis," he stated. "But your secondary degree also includes deep sea excavation and topical mining."

"Yes Sir," she nodded.

His smile widened.

"Your CO at the Navy base on American Samoa spoke very highly of both your deep-sea diving experience as well as your vast knowledge of the underwater topography in the Pacific bed. Especially those around Hawai'i, Guam, and American Samoa."

"That is correct, Sir." She smiled weakly at the Admiral's sincere faith in her abilities. "What would you like me to do, Sir?"

"I need you to study the maps we have and try to narrow down locations these bastards could be using to hide their location until the typhoon passes. I doubt they'll risk moving out of a safe harbor while the eye of the storm is so close," he took a deep breath and considered their options. "Then I need you to figure out the best routes for a small armed Navy vessel to take to rendezvous with SDVT-ONE."

Adrienne stood as the Admiral's assistant approached her carrying a dark blue and white official Navy sweat suit.

"I'll get right on it, Sir."

"Appreciate it, Commander." Jameson turned back to the rest of the officers reviewing primary data as well as the weather updates they were constantly receiving from the World Weather Center.

Keep it together, Adrienne!

She had to help Koa get back safely no matter what. She'd never forgive herself if anything happened to him during her watch.

Forty minutes later a call came in from the communications officer on board the sub informing them that they had reached their coordinates and the SEAL team had just disembarked the vessel.

"Roger that, Lieutenant Kim. I'm verifying your location via satellite. There are no images in your vicinity. Please notify command center after your initial sweep, Lieutenant Choy, out."

"Paul."

Adrienne pointed to a small indentation on the secondary map on the Lieutenant's computer monitor.

"See that area? It's a small inlet with mostly mangrove trees that local fishermen like to use. It's isolated due to the coral reef several klicks away. That's where I'd hide if the US Coast Guard was searching for me."

She arched an eyebrow and sighed when Paul winked at her.

"Good call, Commander." He quickly sent a message to the communications officer onboard the submarine with the coordinates.

"Roger Command, the SEAL team is heading back, and we'll be on our way in less than five minutes, Nemo out."

"How's it going you two?" The Admiral looked hopeful.

"I believe I've found a possible location near their original coordinates, Sir," Adrienne confirmed then pointed at a spot on the display.

"It's only five klicks away," she continued, reviewing the maps in her mind. "It's remote and it's protected by a reef half a klick out so none of our larger ships could reach it directly, and it has mangroves that could easily be used to hide their ship."

"Good work, Commander," Jameson praised. "I'll deploy the back-up unit to those coordinates, hopefully they'll be there."

"How long will it take the unit to reach?" she asked holding her breath.

"An hour and half or so, the wind and rain are really picking up out there." Admiral Jameson left to make the arrangements.

"Adrienne," Paul tugged on her elbow to get her attention, all the while smiling at her. His brown eyes magnified by his glasses. "Go get some coffee. You look wiped-out."

"I will," she replied, muffling a yawn. "As soon as we hear back from them."

Lieutenant Choy nodded, then turned back to monitor the sub's movements. Off to the side, Adrienne waited patiently, admiring how calm and in control Paul was, considering his cousin was out on a mission that included weapons and technologically savvy criminals.

Less than forty minutes later, the com was engaged, and the other officers gathered around Lieutenant Choy's station.

"Go ahead, Nemo," Paul stated calmly.

"The Team just disembarked," the voice informed. "Hostile vessel located at coordinates provided by command central. Area surrounded by thick mangroves, Nemo outside one klick of hostiles. The Team will have to swim a little over a klick to get into the inlet. That's not too far. Not for them."

"How's the weather, Lieutenant?" Admiral Jameson asked, his eyes looking wary.

"Not so good, Sir," the faceless Sailor replied. "The wind is at sixty-one knots. Seas rough and choppy. Nemo is fine, but I don't envy those SEALs out there."

"Thank you, Lieutenant Kim." Admiral Jameson sighed. "Please inform the unit to switch on com links and vid-cams when they arrive, Jameson out."

"Aye-aye, Sir." The voice became silent, leaving the people in the command center on pins and needles as they waited for word from the team heading into a hostile situation.

"It should take them about eight minutes using their underwater propulsion system. They have state-of-the-art equipment, Ma'am. It gives them the upper hand," Paul educated, trying to ease her concern.

They waited tensely, some pacing, some watching Choy monitoring the submarine's location and the progression of the team even though he couldn't see them.

"SEAL Team One should be at the inlet, Admiral," Choy notified as he listened to the information streaming into his headset and over his computer console. Then he engaged the front display screen along with the intercom system so that everyone in the command center could hear the SEAL team as they approached the hostile ship.

Pictures from the video cameras worn by all of the team members came on the front video panel. Then a familiar voice with a Hawaiian lilt through.

"This is Commander Kapahu, checking in."

Adrienne's breath hitched and tears threatened to escape their prison.

"Four hostiles topside; unsure how many below deck not including the Coast Guard hostages." There was a brief silence before Koa whispered, "Going to com silence, Kapahu out."

Then there were only pictures and no commentary as the seven-man team quickly assessed the vessel.

In the conference room, they sat in silence watching the action as the SEAL team surrounded the boat, boarding at different corners of the vessel, looking more like Ninjas rather than sailors. Her heart pounded as she watched Koa board the ship, made his way across the deck taking out two, armed men in his direct path.

Terrified that he would get hurt, Adrienne tried to pretend she was watching a video game in order not to freak out at the violence on the gigantic screen. She had never seen anyone killed before and she prayed she'd never see it again.

A few seconds later, the man she loved, and a couple of his men went below deck. He must have gotten attacked from behind because his camera shook violently from the force of the unseen blow and then all the cameras shut off. They all watched in disbelief as all communications with Koa's SEAL team ceased.

"What the hell is going on?!" the civilian, Mr. Montrose, a weapons consultant hissed. "What happened to the picture? What's going on?"

Lieutenant Choy cleared his throat.

"They must have used a small, low-grade electromagnetic pulse device to take out all of their electronic devices."

"Will it affect the submarine?" Commander Elliot asked calmly.

"No, the range on this particular EMP device is only several yards, the sub is perfectly fine."

Then Choy stopped his commentary and was speaking to someone on a different channel.

"The other team just arrived. They're securing the ship as we speak," he paused, his eyes narrowing, jaw clenched. "Two hostiles secured. The other four deceased. One Coast Guard member was killed by hostiles. His body was left on board the abandoned Coast Guard vessel, but the team is retrieving it. Several wounded."

Then there came another uncomfortable pause.

"Lieutenant Commander Kapahu has been *shot*," his cousin conveyed through clenched teeth, but kept his composure. "Unable to ascertain the severity of his injury."

Adrienne, however, felt the room begin to spin and had to hold on to the corner of Choy's desk to remain upright.

"Commander Mathis?" The Admiral was watching her, concern filling his features. "Are you alright?"

"Yes, Sir," she lied, trying to keep a neutral face.

"Are you sure?" he asked again.

"Yes," she spoke slowly and tried to remember to breathe. "Too much excitement, Sir."

"Or it could be you're worried about Lieutenant Commander Kapahu?" Admiral Jameson smiled.

She choked on her spit and almost knocked over Choy's *Vampire Diaries* pencil holder.

"Pardon me?" she sputtered, still trying to regain her composure.

The older man chuckled.

"The base isn't that big, Commander. People talk," he stated matter-of-factly. "Especially when it concerns a certain single, good-looking, or so I've been told, SEAL team leader who is no longer on the market. You have a lot of females on base up in arms."

She grinned at the man's non-chastising statement.

"That wasn't my intention, Sir," Adrienne blushed against her will.

"Don't worry," Admiral Jameson added. "I met my wife on base too. She was a communication specialist at the time. She was *my* C-O."

"How did they know?" she questioned with sweaty palms.

"Apparently Lieutenant Commander Kapahu has been less *'friendly'* with them and has been caught several times eating dinner and going to the movies with a certain new officer on base. My secretary even claims she saw Lieutenant Commander Kapahu in a jewelry store at the mall picking up an engagement ring."

His eyebrow arched knowingly.

"I'm sorry, but that's classified information," she blushed once more with a smile, all the while wishing a hole would open beneath her and swallow her up.

"I hope he's alright," she whispered it like a prayer.

"I've known my cousin my entire life," Choy chimed in. "The man's too stubborn and too ornery to go down without a fight. Don't worry. The *kolohe* will be just fine."

"Thanks," she inhaled deeply. "I hope you're right."

CHAPTER ELEVEN

Koa knew his whole family was waiting to see him when he got out of surgery, but only his mom and dad were allowed into the ICU.

"Baby boy," his mother whispered into his ear, but he was too groggy to lift his head or move his body. "Everyone is here. They're in the waiting room saying prayers."

"That's right, son," his father's voice came through the haze blanketing his mind. "The doctor said you got hit with one of those, those, penetrating bullets. It hit you in the side, thankfully missing all of your major organs."

"You also have a broken leg," his mother stated with a muffled sniffle.

"The other men said you broke it when one of those bastards tackled you from behind, but they said you still kicked his butt," his father uttered proudly.

He heard his mom's soft voice again and tried unsuccessfully to open his eyes.

"They are gonna keep you in ICU for a few days," she updated him, knowing he would appreciate it. "Then they'll be moving you to a private room upstairs."

"Damn it!" He heard his father swear but couldn't respond. "I wish he'd open his eyes. He looks so pale and fragile like this."

"I know," Leilani, his mom, chuckled nervously. "He's never looked fragile, not even as a baby. He always was intimidating, even though he was such a teddy-bear at heart."

Joseph Kapahu laughed.

"If only those other kids knew his little sister was always beating him up," his dad reminded.

His mom laughed too.

"He would have been so embarrassed," the woman chuckled at his expense.

"He's probably still afraid of her," they both said in unison.

"By the way, son," his father continued. "Adrienne is in the waiting room too. She's worried about you. I have a feeling she's not going anywhere until she knows you're out of danger."

"She's a sweet girl, Koa." His mom squeezed his right hand gently. "Give her a chance to talk to you. I know she loves you, baby boy. She's just scared."

Koa wanted to open his eyes. He wanted to hug his parents and kiss his woman. *His woman*, but the medicine in the IV kicked in again.

Soon, he was drifting peacefully in a dreamworld where he was making slow, mind-blowing love to the woman of his wet dreams... *his woman*... his... wo...

SEALING THE DEAL

"When can I see him?" Adrienne felt her blood pressure rising.

"I'm sorry, Commander," the nurse firmly repeated. "Only immediate family or spouses are allowed in the ICU."

"Of course, she's family," a soft, melodic, Hawaiian lilt came from behind her. "She's my son's fiancée."

Adrienne turned quickly to see Mrs. Kapahu smiling lovingly at her.

"That's alright then," the older nurse winked. "You should have just said so. You two ladies can go on in, but remember, you can only stay for a few minutes."

"Thank you, Ma'am." Adrienne gave the nurse a genuine smile.

"You're welcome," she replied. "You're a lucky woman, Commander. That Sailor is *fine* with a capital *F*."

Adrienne couldn't help the grin that crept over her face.

"Yes, Ma'am."

"How are you holding up, dear?" Mrs. Kapahu asked in a hushed tone when they were out of earshot.

"To tell the truth," Adrienne began. "I'll feel better when he's out of the ICU, and in a regular room."

"I have to warn you, he's a little sleepy," Koa's mother educated. "The medicine is keeping him under, but that's a good thing that way he's not in so much pain."

"Are you sure it's alright to see him?" Adrienne's voice was shaky. "I don't know if he's going to want to see me, Mrs. Kapahu."

"Why wouldn't he want to see you?"

She swallowed, hard.

"I didn't accept his proposal," she mumbled her mistake.

Mrs. Kapahu's brow arched, just like her son.

"I'm sure you had a good reason."

"I'm scared," Adrienne admitted looking down at her feet.

"Then tell him," Mrs. Kapahu urged sweetly. "Let him know your fears. He'll understand."

"But—"

"But nothing," the woman said. "Unless you don't love him."

"I-I'm not sure how I feel," the Commander confided with heated cheeks. "I like spending time with him, but I don't know."

"Well," Mrs. Kapahu replied. "I'm sure that you do, you just don't realize it yet."

"I don't want to upset him."

Leilani frowned.

"Whatever happens in there just remember he's a stubborn, mule headed Kapahu man who speaks first *then* thinks later. Well, as far as women are concerned," the beautiful woman chuckled. "That trait tends to get them in trouble a lot."

SEALING THE DEAL

"Alright," she said, feeling better.

Koa's eyes were closed when they entered the room. His breathing was slow and even, and his ruggedly handsome face softened in sleep giving him an innocent expression. He was mesmerizing even in sleep.

"Go ahead," Mrs. Kapahu urged her into the room. "I'll give you some privacy. Let me know when you're done. Talk to him. The nurses said he can hear us but can't respond."

Then Mrs. Kapahu nodded slowly and closed the door behind her.

Anxiously, Adrienne sat in the chair by Koa's bedside, watching his chest rise and fall under his gown, tempted to pull back the covers and take a peek at his man-goodies. Chuckling to herself, she placed her hand over his. The feel of his large hands so pliant and limp caused tears to form in her already swollen eyes.

"Hey!" she spoke at a regular volume. "It's me Adrienne. I know you're still probably mad at me, but I couldn't stay away."

Sadly, he didn't respond, not even a twitch of a finger. She listened to the steady beeping of the monitor and continued to tell him about what was going on at the base and in the waiting room with his family.

"By the way," she smirked, lightly slapping the hand she was holding. "I met another one of your family members. A very lovely fashion designer who was your *date* to the officer's banquet on base. Needless to say, I was very happy to learn from said fashion designer, who happens to be your cousin, that your sister, Kai, put her up to groping you in order to make me jealous."

Adrienne shook her head and smiled.

"Your sister is very perceptive, but she's also very manipulative." She giggled. "Don't tell her I said that she's a little bit intimidating. Maybe *she* should have been in the military as well."

She spent a few more minutes talking to him and then went to get his mom.

"How is he?" Mrs. Kapahu inquired.

"He's pale but seems to be resting comfortably."

"Good." The woman grinned.

"Mrs. Kapahu?"

"Yes, dear?"

"Could I ask you for a favor?"

"Sure, what do you need?"

Adrienne explained her predicament to Koa's mother and was delighted when she agreed to help her. Excitement fueled her steps as she walked back to her office, feeling more confident in his recuperation. Yes, she was never happier to see someone as much as she was to see him.

She could have stayed there the whole day if she didn't have to fill-out work orders for areas needing to be repaired after the typhoon. Koa looked so peaceful, so childlike; her heart hurt just thinking about him.

During her short time with him in the small hospital room, she memorized every line of his face, even the small scars on his chin and

over his left eye, and the way he snored lightly as he slept, he was so...
Koa. Powerful and intimidating even in his unconscious state. Koa, the name described him completely... *warrior*... and he most definitely was.

It was at that moment the world came screeching to a halt.

She loved him, wasn't just fascinated with him, wasn't in lust with him or his *sexpertise*. Although, that was a wonderful benefit. No. She was in love with the whole man. His intelligence, his playfulness, his gentleness, his ability to stick his foot in his mouth and look adorable doing it.

She loved him all, and as soon as he woke, she would tell him.

Then she would show him just how much she loved him.

CHAPTER TWELVE

Two weeks later...

"Mama," Koa sighed into the telephone receiver, exasperated by his mom's constant harassment. "I've told you before, I'm fine. I don't want you to leave work to take care of me like I'm some sort of infant. I can take care of myself. I'm a big boy now. I even wear big boy underwear."

"Koa Joseph Kapahu," his mother chastised from the other end. "Don't take that tone of voice with me, or I'll take you over my knee. I don't care how old you are."

He chuckled, but as he heard a low growl coming from his mother, his entire body stiffened.

"Sorry, Mama," he quickly apologized. "I know you and the rest of the family are only trying to help."

"That's better," she sighed, and worry laced her words. "If you need me for anything—"

"I'll call I promise."

"*Aloha*, baby boy," the woman's tone softened. "I'll check on you a little later."

"*Aloha*, Mama," he replied, smiling to himself.

Koa hung up the phone and thanked his lucky stars another family member hadn't barged in to help him around the house, deliver food, or just dropped by to keep an eye on him.

Freaking hell!

It was times like these he wished he would have bought that Rottweiler as a guard dog when he had the opportunity.

Koa rolled his eyes, chuckling to himself. He was a Navy SEAL for fuck's sake. He was an expert at Brazilian Jujitsu and hand-to-hand combat. He could operate any handheld weapon on the market. He could hold his breath underwater for over five minutes while disarming a bomb. He spoke four different languages fluently, and his body was considered a deadly weapon, yet his family thought he needed help opening a can of chicken noodle soup.

Whatever!

"Damn it!" He sucked on his thumb when the can opener slipped and cut his index finger.

Knock! Knock! Knock!

Ah hell!

Couldn't they just leave him in peace with his new friend the wheelchair and his DVR episodes of *Hawai'i Five-0*?

Knock! Knock! Knock!

"Keep your pants on!" he yelled at the person on the other side of his front door, banging the wood so hard he thought it might splinter. "What the fu—"

His sentence trailed off as Commander Mathis, *Adrienne*, stood on his front landing, holding a bag, smiling nervously like she'd just done something naughty.

"Hi," she greeted, swallowing hard.

He took a cleansing breath and looked her up and down. His gaze taking in her pretty floral sundress and strappy sandals. He even noticed her chestnut hair falling over her toned shoulders in soft waves. Finally, his gaze rested on her expressive green irises.

"*Aloha*," he finally said. "What are you doing here?"

Nervously, she shifted from one leg to another, holding the brown shopping bag in her hands like it was a case filled with rare and precious gemstones.

"I wanted to check-up on you, make sure you were doing alright," she informed, staring at the trickle of blood slowly leaking from his finger onto the hardwood floor.

Immediately, her mouth gaped, and her gaze widened.

"What the hell?!" Adrienne gasped, stepping into the foyer without formally being asked to enter. "Why are you bleeding? Did your stitches open or something?"

Koa shook his head, smiling at her concern.

"No, it's just an injury I sustained while opening a freaking can of soup."

"Listen to me Koa Joseph Kapahu!"

She was practically yelling now as she ran past him into the kitchen and returned seconds later with a paper towel. Without thought, she wrapped the makeshift bandage around the bleeding digit and squeezed tightly in order to stop the bleeding.

"I know you're a SEAL and some kind of walking superhero, but I want you to let me take care of you, is that clear?"

With a large cheesy grin, he shook his head, sighing under his breath.

"Why?" the injured man poked.

"Why, what?" Commander Mathis snapped with irritation then flew into a rant in French that he understood and that made even him blush. He even touched one of his ears to make sure it was not bleeding.

When she was finished, she ended it with a loud indignant huff.

"Why do you want to take care of me?" Koa asked again, his heart ready to burst. "We barely know each other, remember?"

"I just do," she sighed, and her accent disappeared. After a few minutes, her delicate hands came up defiantly to rest on her well-rounded hips.

"You can take care of me, if you insist," he responded, not able to restrain the smile escaping its confines.

Adrienne's brow rose, eyes narrowing suspiciously.

"Is there another woman here with you?"

"No," he said indignantly.

"There better not be," she grumbled, glancing around as though a naked woman would come out of a hidden door or appear out of thin air.

"There's not, I give you my word." He harassed with a hearty chuckle.

"Good."

Amused at her jealousy, he rolled his eye at her unwarranted paranoia.

"Adrienne, tell me, why are you here?"

She shook the brown bag excitedly.

"What's in the bag?" Koa's annoyance faded and his curiosity took control.

She turned back toward the kitchen, motioning him to follow her.

"Make yourself comfortable," she commanded, while getting two plates out of the cabinet and two forks from the utensil drawer.

Carefully maneuvering around furniture, Koa wheeled himself to the dining table. Then he waited patiently as she unpacked her stash. His frown left and he smiled at her excitement.

"Mmm," he hummed as he eyed the plain brown bag. "You picked up some dinner. Great! I'm starving."

Adrienne shook her chestnut locks *'no'*.

"Even better," she explained, taking out several *Tupperware* containers and placed them on the four-person dinette table. "I cooked!"

"You, cooked?" He felt his eyes widen with shock.

Adrienne had a lot of great assets. She was a formidable fighter who beat him at sparring a couple of times. She was incredibly intelligent and was even more impressive because she had a photographic memory. Her I.Q. was at genius level, and the woman was drop-dead gorgeous. But a good cook, she was not.

"Yes!"

"I thought you said you couldn't cook?" His eyes squinted at the bag and then reminded. "You made lunch for us once, remember?"

"I made salmon." She glared at him.

Koa's face paled.

The woman put the whole fish, scales and all, into a cold pan without seasonings or oil. He ate it though because he loved her and didn't want to hurt her feelings. The next day they both had diarrhea. Thank goodness his house had two bathrooms.

"I'm better now," she pouted. "I've been taking lessons."

"Lessons?"

"Yup, your mom has been teaching me." Adrienne beamed from ear to ear.

Koa grinned sheepishly as he contemplated how *not* to insult her.

"Did she help you with all of this?" His brow arched.

"Nope," she said enthusiastically. "I made all of it by myself."

"Adrienne, I don't wanna hurt your feelings, but I have two fractured ribs. I was shot by a drug-smuggling, gun-wielding maniac, and then lost a butt-load of blood while being transported to the hospital. If you haven't noticed, I'm recuperating from surgery. Did you remember that I was in the ICU for several days?" Then he motioned to his left leg. "I have a broken leg too. I'm not up to par quite yet."

Koa eyed the containers warily.

"Are you afraid?" she asked, trying to contain her laughter.

He rolled his eyes.

"Hell no!"

Her eyes narrowed.

"Yes, I'm terrified," he admitted with fear in his eyes. "I just don't want to get food poisoning on top of all of this."

He waved at his body in frustration.

"C'mon, *puppy*," she teased.

"*Puppy?*"

"Yeah," her words were low and sultry. "That's my new nickname for you."

"Why puppy?" he snickered, feeling better because she was with him.

"Well, why not? You nicknamed me *Kitten*." She grimaced. "Why do you call me that of all things?"

"Because of your beautiful, cat-like eyes and because I like stroking your, you know, your soft little—" He chuckled wickedly.

"Oh, *Oh!*"

Adrienne's face turned from peanut-butter to a shade of deep burgundy.

"That's okay, you'll still be my puppy," she stated firmly when she finally found her voice.

"Why?"

"Because I know how to make you roll over and expose your tummy." She chuckled. "Plus, there are a few more tricks I'd like to teach you."

"Is that right?"

"Mmm, hmm," she continued. "Plus, you also have a tendency to growl."

"Do I?" he blushed.

"Yup!" She snorted but didn't care.

"Now, why are you really here?" he questioned the woman he loved.

She sighed, looking into his expressive hazel eyes.

"When you got shot," she whispered. "I thought my world had come to an end."

Suddenly, she knelt in front of him, looking slightly frazzled.

"Then when you were laid up in the hospital looking all frail and innocent—"

"Absolutely not!" he interrupted. "SEALs don't look frail *or* innocent."

"Anyway, I watched you, lying on that hospital bed, looking all *manly*."

Koa grinned letting her continue.

"And the only thing I could think of was that I might never get to open presents with you on Christmas morning. I might never get to sleep late on a Saturday morning with you, waking up to the sounds of the Pacific lapping against the shoreline. I might never have beautiful Hawaiian French Samoan, Ninja-babies, who surf and make culinary masterpieces while saving people with flat tires and—"

Gently, Koa pulled her onto his lap and placed a finger lightly on her lips. The mere touch eased his restlessness.

"You're rambling again, kitten."

She smiled, leaned in and brushed her lips against his.

"You do that to me, ya big jerk!"

He straightened, his hands beginning to sweat.

"What else do you want me to do to you?"

She paused for a moment.

"I want you to marry me," she propositioned with a hopeful grin.

"Mmm." He placed a hand on the nape of her neck gently rubbing circles over her flawless peanut-butter skin. "I can definitely do that."

"Where's my ring?" she asked breathlessly, green eyes glistening with unshed tears.

"It's in my underwear drawer," he responded, waggling his brows playfully. "The box is hidden underneath my boxer-briefs."

"It figures," she snickered at the idea of rummaging around his underwear drawer.

"Go get it," he encouraged.

Adrienne stood up quickly, ran to the master bedroom and returned a few moments later carrying a small velvet-covered box. She placed it in his hand and waited nervously.

"I love you, Koa Kapahu!" she confessed, feline-shaped green eyes glistening in the waning light. "I love you with everything that I am."

"I love you too, Kitten."

Then he placed the emerald and diamond engagement ring on her finger before tugging her back onto his lap and covering her mouth with a tight, forceful seal. His tongue immediately sought entrance. When she finally relented, he ravished her with deep, wet licks, wicked nips to her lips, and drawing pulls on her sweet, pink tongue. She was delicious and he couldn't wait to marry her and make babies with her.

When they finally came up for air, Adrienne grinned, a slow Cheshire-cat type of grin that made him feel uneasy.

"Why are you smiling at me like that? You're making me *itchy*."

"I've missed your glorious body, that's all." She giggled like a schoolgirl. "You make me feel so… *naughty*."

"Do you want to be *really* naughty?"

She nodded her head yes, and before she could argue, Koa reached under her sundress and pulled off her black silky panties. Without hesitation, he touched her damp folds, caressing and rolling her soft labia between his slightly calloused fingers. A low moan mixed with a sound that resembled a purr escaped her throat making his cock begin to grow inside his sweatpants.

"What about the food?" Adrienne's raspy voice hitched with emotion, urging him on.

He grinned at her response.

"You can poison me later, kitten."

"What are you doing, Lieutenant Commander Kapahu?" she moaned against his lips, while his talented hands drove her to distraction.

"Mmm," he replied, still stroking her now drenched sex while removing his painfully erect member from its confines, and without thought, he placed it at the entrance of paradise.

"I'm sealing the deal, kitten," he whispered as he thrust inside of her tight, wet channel in one fluid glide. "I'm *SEALing the Deal*."

The End!

HAWAIIAN PRONUNCIATIONS

Ali'ikai - *[ah lee 'ee kai]*; King or Queen of the Sea

Aloha - *[ah low ha]*; Love, affection; greeting, salutation; Hello! Goodbye!

Aloha au ia 'oe – I love you.

Haole – *[how lee]*; A foreigner; Pidgin slang – Caucasian

Kapahu – *[kah pah who]*

Koa - *[koh' (w)ah]*; Brave, Bold, Fearless

Kolohe – *[koh' low hee]*; Rascal

Leilani - *[lay lah nee]*; Heavenly Lei; Royal Child

Mahalo – Thank you.

ABOUT THE AUTHOR

L. D. K. Johnson is an American author hailing from the East Coast of the U.S., where she enjoys spending time with family and friends when she is not sitting in front of her laptop writing the next book that comes to mind. Her favorite things in life are chocolate, creamer (not necessarily coffee), and anything D.I.Y. related.

L. D. K. Johnson first made her mark on the writing scene with her beloved contemporary erotic romance books, The Kapahu Series, set on the beautiful Hawaiian island of Oahu. Ms. Johnson followed with Counting Stars, Four Past Midnight, and the first installment of her adult Fantasy series, Lup Teren (Wolf Land Series).

After a several year hiatus from writing, L. D. K. is ready to jump back into the fray; wowing fans with sexy new stories, but not without a reintroduction of her prior books in a new home.

L. D. K. JOHNSON TITLES

AVAILABLE EVERYWHERE!

COMING SOON BY L. D. K. JOHNSON

Project Lieutenant
Episode #3 of The Kapahu Series

Honoring Noelani
Episode #4 of The Kapahu Series

Keeping Keanu
Episode #5 of The Kapahu Series

-ALSO-

LUP TEREN

www.ingramcontent.com/pod-product-compliance
Lightning Source LLC
LaVergne TN
LVHW010300260326
834688LV00044B/1381